Electricland

A Novel by Ginger Mayerson

The Wapshott Press

Electricland

Published by
The Wapshott Press
PO Box 31513
Los Angeles, CA 90031-0513

The Wapshott Press

www.WapshottPress.com

ISBN: 978-0-9825813-1-5

06 05 04 034 3 2 1

Wapshott Press logo by Molly Kiely
Cover design by Robin Austen

There is nothing more dangerous than a woman with nothing to lose.

Electricland

Table of Contents

Chapter 1
Bureaucracy: It's Wonderful.. 1
Chapter 2
Mass Hysteria for Fun and Profit... 11
Chapter 3
Jailhouse Rock 21
Chapter 4
A Policeman's Lot 39
Chapter 5
Detention Doldrums... 47
Chapter 6
Andrew of Baku... 69
Chapter 7
Love is the Greatest Weapon of All... 89
Chapter 8
Attorney Client Privilege 105
Chapter 9
To the Barricades 121
Chapter 10
Sprung in late Spring 133
Chapter 11
Emotional Bankruptcy 149
Chapter 12
A Gun as Lovely as a Tree.. 161
Chapter 13
Here Lie Love's Undiscover'd Mines..................................... 189
Chapter 14
'Tis a Wonder, by Your Leave, She will be Tamed so........... 207

Chapter 1

Bureaucracy: It's Wonderful

Disciplinary action meetings for extramural anti-terrorism units (EAT-U) were held in a secure auditorium-like basement beneath a Virginia shopping mall. It was a grim room, but the middle-aged woman in the baggy tan suit had triumphed so often in rooms even grimmer than this one that it gave her a warm feeling in her thoracic cavity. The room was stuffy, but she was unfazed by it. Her face was a calm, resigned mask, as if she were merely facing another mountain of paperwork in a windowless back office. She wore the Glock 9mm in her shoulder holster as lightly as her cheap wristwatch and pearl stud earrings. She knew she could think her way out of anything, but violence, done well, was sometimes more effective. She was seated across from her abashed Section Manager and his boss, the Department Manager, whom she'd never met before. There were no introductions; they all knew as much as they needed to know about each other and why they were there. And technically, none of them existed outside of discreet payments to secure accounts under approved aliases, so introductions were pointless.

"Okay, Titania, what happened in Los Angeles?" the Department Manager asked.

"The mission went to hell," she said.

"Why?"

"After the Irvine incident, I was instructed to cut back on the kill numbers and, unwisely, I complied," she said, taking a sip of over-roasted coffee purchased from the shop above them.

"Only because wherever your squad goes turns into

a bloodbath," her Section Manager gritted out. "People were beginning to notice."

"It got the results you wanted," she said smoothly. "But there was more to this than just kill numbers. There was romance involved and we were foolishly touched by it. We all were."

The Department Manager gazed at her over his own cup of over-roasted coffee. He'd looked at Titania's personnel file before the meeting. At least he looked at what was available to him on his security level. Based on his reading, he would never have associated the woman before him or her underlings with being foolish, romantic or capable of tender feelings for anything. "And what does that mean?" he asked when the silence went on too long for him.

"I'm sure if we'd not been sentimental and killed Detective Russek before Andrew Ryan was incarcerated or at any time up to his release, this would have all gone more smoothly," she said. "Or at least not as messily as it did."

"Agent Titania," her Section Manager scolded. "This department is not in the business of killing police officers, even Los Angeles police officers, on Federal funding."

"Oh?" Titania sipped her coffee and tried to look interested. "Since when?"

Almost every man in the Los Angeles County Men's Central Jail downtown owed Detective Paul Russek a favor. But there were only a few in there he thought he could trust, and only one he knew he could. And only this one was a nicer guy in jail than out. The double glass between them hardly muted the sneering respect between him and Bishop.

"Fluorescent orange ain't your color, but the shaved head kind of suits you."

Bishop grunted a laugh and waited for Russek to go on. "Hey, I'm living. Who the fuck cares what I wear?" he asked when Russek didn't go on. "You come here to get thanked again for saving my life? Thanks. You can leave now."

"So, I saved your life," Russek said pleasantly, small lines crinkling around his pale blue eyes in a smile. Or an assessing squint; it could be hard to tell if Russek was smiling when he wasn't laughing. "You can return the favor, right?"

"In here?"

"Yeah, actually..." Russek looked embarrassed and annoyed at the same time, but didn't break eye contact. "There's a new guy going to be in your cell in a few days. His name is Andrew Ryan. I want you to keep him safe, like really safe, like you keep your own ass safe."

Bishop raised an eyebrow. "What's he in for?"

"Terrorism."

"Ah, like all the fish lately," Bishop said loftily. "For how long?"

"No idea," Russek said sharply. "Just keep an eye on him."

"He special to you."

"Just kee–"

"You know this place is jam packed with terrorists lately," Bishop casually mentioned. "Ever since that shit went down in Irvine, you coppers are dumping terrorists in here like they was going out of style." He eyed Russek, wondering how far he could push him. Looked like pretty far. "I'm in a two-man cell with four guys, copper, I can barely protect my own self."

"I'll do something about it as soon as I can," Russek grated out. He ran a big hand over his cop-cropped dirty blonde hair. "I'm not God. If I was God, I'd get him into a minimum security facility."

"Why dontcha?"

"They're full up with lawyers on contempt raps after Irvine," Russek said sourly. "I could've told them revoking attorney-client privilege retroactively was gonna suck."

"My lawyer don't have these problems," Bishop said.

"Your fucking shyster only defends thugs. He'd never stoop to defending a mere terrorist." Russek rolled his shoulders. "You gonna help me, Bishop, or not?"

"Okay, okay. I owe ya. I'll keep an eye on this, whatever his name is–"

"Andrew Ryan."

"Yeah, okay." Bishop glanced at the sheriff's deputy standing in the doorway. "Get me a better cell and I'll take good care of him."

"I'll do what I can, but take good care of him no matter what." Russek gave him a hard cop motherfucker look.

Bishop nodded, keeping his face blank. "Hey, sure." He stood and then turned back to Russek. "What so special about this Ryan guy? Might help me protect him to know."

"He saved my life." Russek walked out on those words. He stopped by jail administration to confirm Ryan would be put in with Bishop and add that he wanted them moved to their own cell right away. He was told it would happen as soon as possible; there were truckloads of terrorists coming in since the suspension of *habeas corpus* after the Irvine thing.

Russek went back to the terrorist-hunting headquarters Parker Center had become. He mentally commented for the nth time that the suspension of *habeas corpus* would have suited its namesake, the gung-ho ex-marine Chief William H. Parker, down to the ground. In the 1950s Parker had militarized the LAPD to the point they were almost as dangerous as the criminals. His successors had continued the tradition that crime was not a problem to be solved, but an enemy to be annihilated. Due process was a mere annoyance for the crusaders the LAPD put in charge over the decades. They had paid a heavy price for it occasionally, but not often enough for any real change in the cop mindset. The most recent Chief of Police had tried to undo some of this mindset, but history was against him. Terrorism was now the enemy, and the Irvine thing had given the LAPD a green light to arrest everyone in sight and work countless hours of overtime doing it.

This wouldn't be a problem for Russek; he'd been a cop long enough to just do his job and forget about it when he went home. Except now at home there was Drew and in spite of all Russek's protests and affidavits, the State of California had decided Drew was a terrorist and must be put into custody. In a moment of pure frustration, Russek had considered making a run for Mexico, but then they might both end up in a Mexican jail awaiting extradition. No, the best thing was to make the best of it in LA, where Russek at least had some strings to pull. And he would pull all of them to save Drew, who'd saved his life and returned his love.

Another guy who'd once saved Russek's life was Warren Williams. At least that was the name he was going by in Afghanistan when Russek got hauled back onto active duty and ran into an independent contractor named Warren Williams. Tall, dark, handsome, suave, lethal: Williams had thrown Russek to the ground and covered him with his body when some lunatic in a burka opened fire on a crowded street. Williams had a sixth sense for trouble, which was why he was still alive. And Russek had admired that and valued Williams' friendship right up until he drove Russek's car into a situation that nearly killed him.

Of course Russek had been happy to see Williams on his front porch one evening almost a year after they'd parted in Kabul. "Goddamn, Warren, you haven't changed at all," he'd said, letting the mercenary into his home. "Drink?"

"Sure, and I'd be much obliged if you'd let me flop on your couch for a day or two," Williams drawled. "I'm in transit."

"Hell yes you can stay here," Russek said, getting out the good scotch. "Where're you in transit to?"

"Difficult to know, I haven't got my marching

orders yet," Williams said, settling onto the couch he'd be sleeping on. "Iran, probably, but maybe Pakistan."

"Your life's very exciting." Russek sat in the armchair next to the couch.

"Too exciting sometimes." Williams smiled coolly. "Heard you had some excitement in Irvine lately. It took hours to get through security at LAX."

"Oh, Jesus, we did." Russek ran his hand over his eyes. "Forty thousand dead, hospitals, morgues, emergency services overwhelmed. I had to go down there with a squad to help keep order; I only drank Cokes and Gatorade for three days. And the DHS still doesn't know what the poison was or how the poison got into the water supply or if there's any left in it or if it will turn up in LA water. We had bottled water riots a few days ago."

"I heard," Williams said sympathetically. "You worried?"

"Not really." Russek flashed his crooked smile. "I figure when your number's up you gotta go. Whether it's getting offed by some punk or poisoned tap water, that's how it is. I drive on the freeway, too, so I'm either a lucky sumbitch or it just ain't my time yet."

"One can't worry about these things." Williams agreed. "Gets in the way of living while you can. Any idea who done it?"

"No, just a rumor that an old woman's car broke down near the reservoir just before the event," Russek said. "No one can remember anything about her except she was old."

"Old or middle-aged?" Williams asked.

"What's the difference?"

The next day, Russek didn't have a moment's hesitation in lending Williams his car because he had a police vehicle he could use. He'd just jokingly asked him to gas it up, which was a pretty expensive request that spring. It was only when Williams didn't bring it back that night that he'd started to wonder what was going on. At one AM, Russek called the station to ask them to run the LoJack location. He didn't recognize the address in the South Bay, but it was odd enough that he asked some local cops to meet him there.

It was more than odd, it was an ambush. Arriving at the deserted industrial park, Russek and the local cops were driven into the boxy glass and stucco building by gunfire. More gunfire inside; Russek dove into an office where he found a skinny young guy with long brown hair and big brown eyes working frantically on a laptop under a desk.

"Oh, my God, who are you?" the kid asked in a panicked whisper and white as a sheet.

"LAPD, who–?"

"Can you get me out of here?"

"Yeah, if I can get myself out of here," Russek hissed back.

They made their way into other offices; every corridor led to a dead end, or worse, shots out of nowhere. At one point, the boy picked up a stray gun and shot one of the shadows about to shoot Russek. "Thanks, kid," Russek said, genuinely touched.

"You're welcome, just– let's go!" The kid was very quietly having a nervous breakdown.

Russek's cop-hearing picked up the sirens before the kid did. He huddled with him behind some file cabinets and knew they'd be okay in a few minutes. "What's your name, kid?"

"It's not kid, it's Drew, Drew Ryan. Let's get–"

"Drew? What's that short for?" Russek whispered, pulling the fidgety, shaking kid into his arms, mainly to keep him quiet.

"Andrew." Drew calmed down a little once Russek had his arms around him. "This is a weird time for introductions, but, you? Who are you?"

"Paul Russek. Detective. Hear those sirens?" Russek asked, his lips very close to Drew's ear. "We're gonna be okay. What were you doing in here?"

"I'm an IT consultant–"

"A what?"

"Computers. I work on computers," Drew said barely audibly under the gunfire around them and the heavy boots of the LAPD SWAT team storming the building. Russek got out his cell phone and called headquarters to tell them to relay his presence, location, and to not shoot him or the witness with him.

At the precinct, Russek waited until Drew made his statement, which was simply that he was supposed to meet his friend John Reid at the building to discuss a computer job, and then hid from the burglars when the shooting started. Except, as Russek learned while making his own statement, they weren't garden variety burglars, they were heavily armed Samoan girls. At least the dead ones they found when the smoke cleared were. And what they were after in an inconspicuous office building that he later learned was a DARPA front was still a mystery.

"I know your lock-up is jammed with terrorists," Russek explained to the precinct captain. "So I'm taking him home with me. If that's a problem, then I'll arrest him and he'll be in my custody."

"Shit, Russek, he's a witness, not a suspect," the captain spat at him. "Take him to Disneyland for all I care. I couldn't get him in our lock-up with a shoehorn anyway. Go home, go away. But he stays where he can be questioned. You know the drill."

"Yeah, I do," Russek thought as he collected Drew and drove home in his unmarked police car. His private car had been impounded, which was annoying, but not the end of the world.

"Wh-where are we going?" Drew asked in the car.

"My place."

"Why?"

"You wanna go to your place?" Russek asked, slowing the car down.

"No, I...I'm in a hotel, I just have a few things..."

"New in town? Okay, let's get your stuff," Russek said, sounding like he was in charge and this was the best possible idea. Drew didn't argue; soon he had his suitcase, was checked out and on his way to Russek's tiny house on a Silverlake hillside.

"You can sleep on the couch, which isn't so comfortable," Russek said when they arrived. "Or you can sleep with me. You still look a little freaked out."

"I feel very freaked out," Drew admitted, following Russek into his bedroom.

They didn't become lovers that night, but it was inevitable from the moment Russek put his arms around the shaking kid to calm him down in the shoot-out. Russek had fallen deeply in love with Drew.

Chapter 2

Mass Hysteria for Fun and Profit

"At what point did you lose control of Williams, Titania?" The Department Manager looked at his notes in his own numeric code.

"I never had control of him," she said, looking at her perfectly manicured nails. "He was the CIA's problem, but even they couldn't control him. He was a loose cannon all the way around."

"How the hell did he end up in the DARPA building?" her Section Manager asked. His voice was squeaky with suppressed rage, bordering on panic; that had always annoyed her about him.

"Williams was smart, in a crude sort of way. He picked up Viola's trail in Afghanistan and followed her to Baku, where she was making contact with that damn Ryan child."

"What was Ryan doing in Baku?" the Department Manager asked. He had it in his notes but he wanted some elaboration. "Other than playing computer games with your team?"

"He was running drugs on the internet," Titania said. They stared at her. "I'm hardly an expert, but I understand that that's how it's done these days," she went on when they continued to stare at her. "It's all online logistics now," Titania said with a sigh. Running drugs had never appealed to her. There were too many variables in each transaction for her team to get a successful revenue stream from it. They could barely cope with Hermia's modest weapons-and-drug operation in Laos. "Point to point arrangements, heavily scrambled on all ends, so only the little people and mules get caught, which is surprisingly seldom. The parts of Central and Southeast Asia the drugs run in are in such chaos, there's really no such thing as law enforcement anymore. Of course, getting the drugs into the U.S. is trickier if you don't have a contact in the military or a big contractor to bring them in."

"I suppose you mean like your organization?" her Section Manager practically sneered at her.

"Ah, no, we're a very small shop compared to those kinds of organizations. Not big enough at all for that kind of thing," she said, mentally adding, "And you're not big enough to manage the big extramural drug operations." Keeping the country slightly destabilized through terror was one set of skills; keeping it messed up, but functional on drugs, was another set. Titania knew well enough one should play to one's strengths and not dwell on, but be aware of, one's weaknesses.

"What was Ryan's involvement in the Los Angeles incident?" the Department Manager asked bringing the conversation back to the issue at hand.

Titania took a deep breath so she would say what needed to be said and not a word more or less. The last thing she wanted to admit was that Miranda, her internet specialist, had been stupid and arrogant, which was partly why they'd been in such a mess in Los Angeles. "Although we have enhanced access to networks through our paton, Mr. Cheney, my cyber operative likes to use gamers as cyberterrorists in what's called Electricland," she said carefully. "They think it's a game, but it's not. We only use gamers in obscure parts of the world where they won't see the effects of what they're doing. These gamers are mostly idiots, but occasionally you get a smart one, a hacker–"

"Like Ryan in Baku?" the Department Manager asked.

"Yes and no. Ryan was a gamer in Baku, which is pretty obscure. But, no, unlike Ryan because Ryan is even smarter than the usual smart hacker/gamer we like to run online," Titania said patiently. "He was smart enough or stupid enough to hack into our network and—"

"I thought that couldn't be done!" the Section Manager squeaked.

"So did we," Titania said coolly. "But one learns something new every day."

It had taken the kid a few days to calm down and feel comfortable around Russek. On their first night together nightmares had sent Drew scrambling for his inhaler. Russek could only hold him lightly until the kid could breathe easily again. Eventually the nightmares subsided, but a new nightmare began to loom over them: Drew had been reclassified from witness to terrorist. Only Russek and a few others knew this and Russek had managed to convince everyone around him that it was absurd. For the moment they were allowing Russek to keep Drew with him under house arrest (although Drew didn't know it), but the pressure was mounting from the Feds to move the kid into any lock-up available. Russek had been able to stall, bully and maneuver the system into putting Drew in LA Men's Jail where he'd be close and Russek could call in a few favors to keep him safe until he could get him out. If he could get him out: there was that to worry about.

They'd become lovers a few days after Russek brought him to his place. After a long day policing, Russek came in bone tired and disgusted. But Drew had smiled, the first relaxed and happy smile Russek had ever seen on him, and said, "Welcome home." Russek's usual manly clap on the shoulder became a caress as Drew leaned into it and became an embrace that became a long sweet kiss, seemingly of its own accord.

"Sorry," Russek said, leaning back to put a little space between them and get a good look at Drew's face.

Drew closed the distance and nestled in his arms, face buried in Russek's shoulder. "I'm not."

They moved to the couch to make out and talk a little before anything irrevocable happened. The kid was practically a virgin; he'd only made love a couple of times, and that was with some older guy in Baku. "Baku? Where's that?" Russek asked.

"Azerbaijan," Drew said. "On the Caspian Sea," he continued when he got a blank look. "Kind of between the Middle East and Russia."

"Oh, what were you doing there?" Russek asked, nibbling on Drew's earlobe. "Don't tell me, " he whispered. "IT consulting." He smiled against Drew's nod. "That's a long way from here. How'd you get there?"

"My mom was a secretary with the Embassy in Prague," Drew said, tilting his head to give Russek better access to his neck. "She brought me over when I finished college, but we didn't get along so well, so I split and wandered around until I landed a job in Baku."

"How old are you, Drew?" Russek asked, holding him closer.

"Twenty-four."

"Girlfriends?"

"Just this older lady once," Drew said. "In Baku."

"You didn't get a lot of action in Baku," Russek observed.

"I got all my action in Baku," Drew said wryly.

"Tell me about this guy."

"He was very gentle and careful, used a condom and didn't rush," Drew said, breathless at the memory. "I really liked him and...I really liked, y'know, it."

"It?" Russek asked.

"Sex with a guy. I mean, if I had to choose, that's what I'd want to do."

"Good, so you know what to expect?" Russek asked and Drew nodded. "What happened to this guy?"

"I was supposed to meet up with him at that building," Drew said softly. "But I met you instead."

"Lucky me." He took Drew by the hand and led him to bed.

The kid was shy; Russek found that endearing as he pulled the oversized t-shirt and baggy jeans off him.

His skin had an unhealthy pallor, but was smooth and warm to the touch. "You need more sun and exercise, Drew," Russek said, turning the light off.

"I hate going outside," Drew murmured between gasps as Russek tweaked his nipples. "Ow."

"Ow?"

"Not so hard." The kid pressed his thin lips to Russek's.

"You're fragile," Russek whispered against Drew's mouth, and got a sexy giggle for an answer. "But this is all right," he added, stroking pre-come down the length of Drew's rock hard penis. The kid moaned and arched against him, and fumbled for Russek's half-mast cock. "No," Russek sighed. "This is about you tonight."

Pulling Drew astride his groin, Russek encouraged the kid to kiss him and grind their erections together. A quick study, Drew was soon voluptuously rubbing them together while his tongue explored Russek's mouth and his fingers pinched the older man's nipples. "Does that hurt?" Drew asked breathlessly.

"No." Russek flipped open the lubricant.

"Would you like it to?"

"No." Russek pulled Drew down for a kiss with one hand while the other explored his ass with slick fingers.

Drew wiggled happily against the fingertip inside him, sliding his erection against Russek's and really getting into it when Russek worked two fingers inside. "Paul...I want...oh!" The kid squeaked with pleasure when Russek hit his sweet spot. "That...yeah, that..."

"Oh, that..." Russek teased as he rolled a condom down his cock and lubed it. He arranged Drew face down with a pillow under his hips. "Comfy?" he asked, his cock nudging at Drew's asshole.

"Mmmm..." Drew sighed and then gasped when Russek pressed the head in.

"Ow?" Russek asked, really hoping he wouldn't have to stop.

"A little," Drew admitted. "Go slow, okay?"

"I will," Russek said, kissing Drew's sweaty shoulders. "You're really tight."

"I've...only done this a few times," Drew said, almost imperceptibly arching his ass.

Russek sank in another centimeter. "It's all right, baby, you're doing great," he whispered against Drew's ear. "Try to push me out."

"What?"

"Just do it," Russek said, and he pushed farther in as the pressure around his cock eased.

"Oh...I..." Drew was breathing hard and moaning softly into the pillow.

"Let me hear you," Russek said, reaching around to stroke Drew's cock back to full hardness while he pushed all the way in. "Hey, we made it," Russek panted. He got a cross between a low animal growl and a whimper as he started, very gently, to move inside Drew. Neither of them lasted very long: Drew had a hard, howling climax in Russek's hand. Russek had a kinder, gentler orgasm from Drew's clenching around him, which was kind of disappointing because Russek had wanted to fuck him more. Well, there was always next time, which would be, he hoped, very, very soon.

After they cleaned up, Drew fell asleep like a sweet, trusting babe in Russek's arms. Russek stroked his mahogany hair off his forehead and had a moment of pity for the man who'd lost this wonderful kid by being stupid. And then he thanked his lucky stars he'd lived long enough to find this powerful love with this beautiful young man.

The next morning, Russek took the kid to Astro's Restaurant for a nice breakfast.

Kate parked the car-jacked Lexus a little ways down the street from Russek's place, but with a good view of the house. "Not bad for a love nest," she said, her voice betraying her years in London. It was her relaxed or swanky voice; just then she was with a comrade and felt safe.

"How you know they're doin' it?" Helena in the passenger seat asked.

"I wired it for sound yesterday." With black hair and the right attitude, Kate could pass her middle-aged Middle Eastern looks off as a Latina. That is, if no one looked too hard, and at her age, no one was ever looking too hard. "Russek uses a cleaning service. That bloody kid hardly noticed me as I cleaned around the little bastard. Didn't even look away from his laptop. The audio's been nicely steamy so far. Have a listen?" Kate held out an iPod and earbuds.

"Nah, not unless there's something more useful in it than smut."

"So far Miranda, Titania and Hermia haven't heard anything of use," Kate said, shoving the iPod back in her pocket. "But they're getting an earful of rumpy pumpy."

"Whatever that is," Helena muttered, staring out the window shield.

"Sex," Kate told her.

"Fucking Miranda!" Helena recrossed her legs and looked like she wanted to bite something or someone. "This is all her fault."

"I blame Williams more." Miranda had bailed Kate out more than once, so she was reluctant to go against her. "And this sodding Ryan kid. I detest smart kids."

"Yeah, you right. Why didn't you finish what Viola screwed up when she laid Ryan instead of killing him like she was supposed to?" Helena asked. She was pissed off that she had to be there to help clean up a mess not of her own making.

"It's more complicated now," Kate said with a sigh. "The little bugger had enough time to get away with more than the accounts and passwords. He grabbed some DARPA data we were using as well."

"Sheee-yit." Helena had lost everything to Katrina but her Ninth Ward drawl on certain words. "Can't do nothing 'bout the DARPA stuff. I wish Titania and Miranda would stop fucking with people who are fucking scarier than us, it's just fucking stupid. And can't Miranda just change fucking the passwords or whatever the fuck she does on the internets?"

"I'm told that would tip off our funding sources," Kate said, in a soothing voice. She was mildly amused by Helena's rage and relieved she wasn't holding it in. Helena didn't have a rage meter; it was more like an on-off toggle. "And the DARPA stuff, well, they had the best possible toxin and plans to poison a small city. No sense reinventing the wheel, you know."

"Only if your goddamn wheel doesn't run over your goddamn self. Hey, girl, quit laughing."

"Sssorry." Kate could barely get this out between chuckles.

Helena stared into space while Kate collected herself. "How'd Williams get to DARPA before you?" she asked when her comrade was under control. "I thought this was supposed to be easy. Just get in, flip the switch and follow Miranda's instructions on getting our footprints off the DARPA network or whatever you were supposed to do?"

"Fucking Miranda left a chink for the Ryan kid to get in and Williams had a way we don't totally understand yet to wedge it open," Kate admitted. "Miranda thought she was IMing me when she was IMing the kid."

"Aw, Christ inna Cadillac."

"Indeed. I was delayed by the chaos in Irvine, and then by Miranda not being able to get past the new DARPA security—because you know they'd never admit it, but DARPA knew right away what happened—and then I had no idea the building would be more or less empty, which I think was more Williams voodoo–"

"You just say voodoo, girl?"

"No offense to voodoo or even hoodoo, luv," Kate said pacifically. "I didn't know what kind of resistance to expect, so organizing the Samoan girls held me up a bit."

"Your girl ganstas weren't much help?" Helena

asked. She preferred to work alone and looked askance at Kate's teambuilding efforts. Of course Kate's team members didn't get to live very long after the mission, but it was still too many variables, too many trails to follow, for Helena's taste.

"Oh, they're appropriately vicious and they can shoot straight enough, but they have to see it coming at them." Kate tapped on the steering wheel and stared into the middle distance. "But Williams has nearly the same training that we have," she continued. "He hunted us through the building, picked the girls off one by one. It went pear-shaped. I couldn't get a bloody thing done in there. But Russek's too-smart-for-his-own-good boy-toy stashed the data he'd stolen somewhere and could screw us all if Russek gets it."

"Why you think Russek ain't got it already?"

"We're still a going concern, aren't we?" Kate said.

Helena sighed, drew her Mauser and screwed a silencer on it. "So, here we are. Let's just kill 'em both and get it over with," she said, her voice softening in anticipation of action. "You know that's what Titania will want eventually."

"Ah, but Titania wants us to wait," Kate said, sorry to disappoint Helena, who, like herself, was at her best when killing people. "She and Miranda don't quite know what they've lost and the only way to get it is from Ryan. We might have to beat it out of the little beast."

"Oh. Well, that might be fun." Helena stared at a rectangle of light in the garden across the street from them.

"Thanks for coming to help," Kate said, also watching the garden.

"It's my pleasure to drop everything and come out to this hellhole for you, sugar."

"Sorry things are so cocked up," Kate continued, still watching at the garden. "Isabella might join us." A medium-sized dog trotted to the fence and stared at their borrowed car, perhaps smelling the decaying owner in the trunk with its superior canine olfactory bulbs.

"It's not a massacre without Isabella," Helena observed. "Sit back a bit, hon," she said when the dog began to bark. Leaning across Kate she shot the dog, which dropped without a sound. "I hate dogs. Let's go."

Chapter 3

Jailhouse Rock

The Department Manager consulted the pad he was doodling on. At least Titania assumed they were doodles. They might be code; the man was no fool as far as she could tell based on her limited acquaintance with him.

"Afghanistan," he said with a sigh. "I am so sick of things going so wrong in Afghanistan. And what the hell was Viola doing in Afghanistan that Williams could tail her to Baku and Ryan? Your funding is mostly as a domestic terror organization."`

At this point in the discussions, it was necessary for Titania to carry on a dual train of thought so she didn't let anything slip.

"Yes, we're primarily a domestic operation, but occasionally we have to work outside the county," she said. "Our funding is flexible on that point, as long as our actions cause instability within the U.S. or U.S. spheres of influence abroad."

"Only four of us can stand to live in the United States full-time. The other three only come in for missions," she thought. "I can only stand it if I don't go out very much or watch Fox News or read the New York Times or blogs or Doonesbury."

"So what was Viola doing in Afghanistan?" The Department Manager was a dogged questioner. Titania might have admired that if it wasn't directed at her.

"She was there to back up Kate in killing Williams," she said. "My team usually works alone, but this was unusual. Kate wanted to minimize the damage. There were civilian and military in the area to consider."

"When Kate saw Williams with American soldiers, she knew she'd need back-up," she thought. "Tactically wise, but ultimately futile. That bastard has a sixth sense for people trying to kill him."

"And what happened?" her Department Manager asked. She sent him reports that were so vague and convoluted that he'd probably read what happened, but couldn't fess up that he hadn't understood a word of it.

"Well, we missed," she said. "And Williams recognized Viola from another mission that overlapped with his. Before he went rogue, if indeed he has gone rogue, there was a time when we could work quite amicably with his department."

"We really screwed it' up. Viola thought Williams wouldn't recognize her under the burka when she tried to knife him in the souk. Foolish woman, that man never forgets a face, a figure or a perfume," she thought. "Especially not Viola's."

"And what was Williams interfering with that required two operatives to fail to assassinate him?"

"Periodically we like to catch medium-sized terrorists for show trials in the United States," she said. "This affords them an opportunity to spout off about the vast,

"We were protecting Hermia's drugs and arms operations," she thought with great bitterness. "Williams learned she'd survived the interrogation he'd abandoned her to when

well-funded worldwide terrorist organizations with their sights set on the complete destruction of the U.S., ready to swoop down and destroy our way of life."

he ran away from the mission, the bastard. He was there sniffing out how she was running drugs and guns in southeast Asia. This annoyed me very much."

"And how was he interfering with your operations?" the Department Manager asked.

"He was in position to tip off our target subjects in the region," she said.

"He was in a position to disrupt our opium route into Laos," she thought.

"Why would Williams do that? I thought he was working with the CIA," he asked.

"So did they," she said. "But he's been working for whoever pays the most for a long time now. I mentioned this some time ago to a contact in the CIA and was ignored."

"They're such idiots at the CIA," she thought. "Every now and then, they're useful idiots, but mostly they're just bumbling lethal idiots to be avoided at all costs."

"Well, hindsight is 20-20, Titania, and since technically, you and your group don't exist, there really was no reason for anyone at Langley to take you seriously," her Section Manager babbled.

"Yes, I understand completely," she said. "Even though I was completely right about him."

"Those fools don't listen to anyone until it's too late," she thought. "And they never admit they're wrong."

"So...how did Williams get to Ryan in Baku via Viola?" the Department Manager asked.

"He followed her. I sent Viola up to Baku to reason with that Ryan child," she said. "I dearly hoped we could resolve the little situation he'd stumbled upon in Electricland amicably, possibly even give the lonely boy a job and a feeling of belonging."

"I sent her up there to kill him, but she decided to seduce him first," she thought, annoyed again with Viola's romantic nature. "If she'd killed him the day she arrived, he wouldn't have been sexually confused and a sitting duck for Williams to seduce and run off with."

"And how did it go wrong?" the Department Manager said, doodling oh so casually.

"Once Williams, using his John Reid cover, saw that Ryan was Viola's target, he convinced the boy to go to Istanbul with him and we lost them there," she said.

"Williams is a cunning, sexy bastard when it's useful to him," she thought. "Once Ryan got a taste of Williams' manlove, that stupid hacker would have done anything for him."

"John Reid? Why is that name so familiar?" her Section Manager asked, trying to make it sound like a profound question.

"It's a common name," she said. "They're both very common names.

"It's the Lone Ranger's real fictional name," she thought.

"Why was Williams after Ryan?" her Department manager asked.

"Williams didn't know why we wanted Ryan, just that we did, and that was enough motivation to grab him and vanish," she said. "Especially since we'd just unsuccessfully tried to kill him; he was looking for some kind of lever to get back at us. He hit the fucking jackpot with Ryan. If you'll pardon my language."

"Williams had decided that it was kill us or be killed by us," she thought. "He deduced that Ryan must be a new kind of threat to us, a fluke, an anomaly, a loose end of tremendous power because the boy was such a bumbling nonentity in person. Viola has decidedly odd taste in men. She thought Ryan was coltishly charming in bed."

"And Williams brought Ryan into the U.S. to the DARPA front. Why?" the Department Manager asked.

"Our unit tries not to waste money by using existing resources," she said. "We knew DARPA had a water-poisoning plan and all the supplies for a small city on tap, so to speak, in that South Los Angeles front. So we stole it and used it for the Irvine operation. Williams, via Ryan hacking into Miranda's network, knew we'd be in that building covering our tracks. I'm not sure what he planned to gain by being there."

"We were very unwise to mess with DARPA," she thought. "Why in God's name did we ever think we could get away with it? Why? And then Miranda was distracted when the simple covering-our-tracks operation became a cop magnet and she didn't notice Ryan in her network, copying the data on half our funding streams and God knows what else. And what did he do with it? Neither Williams nor the LAPD have it, so where on earth is it?"

"I've read the LAPD reports on the issue, so you needn't go into the aftermath of the failed mission," her Department Manager said. "What actions did you take to secure Ryan, Russek and Williams?"

"While Ryan was in jail, he was unavailable to us," she said. "We assumed Russek was a dead-end because if Ryan had told him anything, the LAPD would have done something stupid by then. But, on the off chance Russek did know something, and the fact that killing policemen is frowned upon, we kept him under surveillance but otherwise kept our distance. Williams vanished, but we knew he'd surface eventually. So we waited."

"While Ryan was in jail, he was unavailable to us," she said. "We assumed Russek was a dead-end because if Ryan had told him anything, the LAPD would have done something stupid by then. But, on the off chance Russek did know something, and the fact that killing policemen is frowned upon, we kept him under surveillance but otherwise kept our distance. Williams vanished, but we knew he'd surface eventually. So we waited."

"And waited and waited and waited and waited," she thought, seething inside, but maintaining her government-contractor professional cool on the outside.

"Up against the wall!" Deputy A slammed Bishop against said wall, kicked his feet apart, and patted him down while another deputy watched the very uncurious jailhouse crowd in the corridor. "Your new cellie moves in tonight," the deputy said in a low voice over Bishop's shoulder.

"I get a new cell?" Bishop asked, barely moving his lips.

Never taking his eyes off the inmates streaming in front of them, Deputy B said, "We're workin' on it. We're past capacity and administration shoehorns two more guys in here. Russek's pal and some other guy."

"Anyone I know?" Bishop asked.

"Maybe," Deputy B pantomimed firing a gun, the jailhouse gesture for an armed robbery or assault with a deadly weapon rap. Either made this guy a man, not a punk, and definitely not a terrorist. "I don't mind helping Russek," the deputy went on. "He saved my life once."

"He that kind of guy," Bishop observed.

"But we get anymore bodies in here, we're gonna have to break out the Wesson Oil to get 'em in the cells at night."

Bishop nodded and moved off without saying anything when Deputy A shoved him in the direction the rest of the inmates were headed. Later that day a gangsta he knew introduced Bishop to a big guy named Samsa in the yard. Samsa had cold black eyes, a nose that had been broken at least once, and a lean and hungry look (the phrase just rolled into Bishop's brain from nowhere) in a crowd of starving, vicious men. Samsa had cigarettes, but Bishop didn't smoke. Samsa also had gum, which Bishop refused even though he did chew gum. There was something not quite right about the guy, but Bishop couldn't put his finger on it.

"I heard ya know how to handle yourself in here," Samsa said, putting the gum back in his orange jumpsuit pocket.

"Nah, I'm just a thug," Bishop said and walked away diagonally so he could keep this Samsa person in his peripheral vision. Later in the mess hall, Samsa ended up at a table near Bishop, who could not fail to notice how much space the other inmates gave him. Even with staggered meal times, they were shoulder to shoulder at the tables, but this Samsa guy had more elbow room than anyone else. He was either a bad motherfucker or...or what? A cop would be dead by now, so if he was a cop, he must be one seriously bad motherfucker cop.

Andrew Ryan arrived on Bishop's overcrowded tier amid catcalls and whistles. "Shit," Bishop thought when he caught sight of the kid at the end of the tier. Even with a shaved head and the unbecoming fluorescent orange jumpsuit, the kid was adorable. And this, Bishop was sure, would make protecting the little punk a nightmare.

The deputy shoved Ryan into the cell and pointed at Bishop, "That's your new best friend," and walked away.

Drew's eyes widened. "Are you–?"

"Get in the bottom bunk and shut up," Bishop said. He leaned against the bunks, obscuring anyone's view of who was in the bottom one. He had to repeatedly growl at Drew to shut up until the kid got the message that he should speak only when spoken to.

Bishop stood over Drew in his bunk while the stream of curious jail residents got a look at the fish. At least a look at what they could see; standing in front of his bunk like that Bishop was broadcasting that this was his fish. Bishop had a reputation for not looking for trouble, but for being a very bad ass motherfucker when crossed. And although he bought the occasional blowjob, he wasn't one for domestic arrangements, so if this kid was more than a cellie, which by being in Bishop's bunk certainly seemed the case, this was a kid to steer way far clear of. At least that's what flew through the jailhouse grapevine ten minutes after Drew curled up in Bishop's bunk.

The truth was simpler: there were now five guys in a two-man cell. "When you call Russek, you tell him to get us moved yesterday," Bishop growled over his shoulder and then went back to staring down his fellow inmates.

Samsa stopped at the cell door, glanced at Drew and offered Bishop some gum, which was refused. "So, how's it–?"

"Where you on your way to, Samsa?" Bishop asked, not moving from in front of his bunk.

"Uh, the yard, I just–"

"I'll see you there," Bishop said, face blank, arms loose at his sides, but lower body was in a fighting stance, ready to spring at the slightest provocation.

Sensibly, Samsa left without another word.

Bishop relaxed and looked down at Drew, who was looking around his new environment with a stunned expression. "You Andrew Ryan, right?" he asked and got a scared nod back. "They call ya Andy or Andrew?"

"D-Drew," the kid managed to say. "They call me Drew."

Bishop sat next to him on the bunk. "You trust Russek, right?" Bishop asked. He got another scared nod. "Good, cause I trust him, too," he went on. "So you gotta trust me and do what I say. And the first thing is that you keep your eyes down and your mouth shut. You look at me and no one, and I mean no one else, or I will kick your ass." Bishop paused to let that sink in. "There's five of us in this cell now." Drew's eyes widened. "You sleep in this bunk with me until Russek gets us moved, understand?" Drew nodded and looked scared. "You sleep with your back to the wall and I sleep in front of you, understand?" Drew nodded, still looking scared. "You listen to me, I keep you safe. You don't listen, every mutherfucker in here will take a piece out of you, understand? Repeat it back to me." Bishop listened to a very accurate recital of what he'd just said, not word for word, but acceptable. "So, relax, it could be worse."

"How?" Drew asked.

"Eyes down, mouth shut!" Bishop glared at him because he really didn't know how it could be worse for either of them.

"Ain't Ryan scheduled for some interrogation in that jailhouse? The CIA or FBI or DHS must be in there, why not slip one of us in?" Helena asked over the secure line Miranda had routed through the IRS, of all places. Even if tax preparers were listening, it wouldn't make a bit of sense to them.

"Russek's friends in the jail are keeping Ryan off the interrogation list," Titania said. "I know this because I tried to get the CIA and DHS to him put on the list and even they got stonewalled. This Russek character is either well loved or deeply feared or both."

"Let's kill Russek," Helena suggested. "It'd be easy, he ain't paying much attention to anything but his jailbird loverboy."

"Let's wait, Helena, Russek might be useful one day...somehow," Titania said reasonably.

"Maybe you right. Then let's hire someone in there to kill Ryan," Helena said reasonably. "Or that might happen anyway; I hear they're stacked up like kindlin' in that place."

"I'm not ready to give up on him," Titania said with a sigh. "Yet."

"Well, don't fret, Titania honey, we can always get him when he gets out."

"Who said he's getting out?" Titania asked, more annoyed than consoled by Helena's consolation. She could shove her conso–

"Russek an' them in LA." After getting the last word, Helena hung up like she always did.

Titania didn't worry about things. She didn't fret or angst or agonize or fuss or, God forbid, get upset. She brooded, pondered and mulled in what she hoped was an elegantly intelligent manner. But never for very long because it really was a complete waste of time. Rising from her desk, she put on her suit jacket and walked down the hall to Miranda's freezing lair.

Titania's offices occupied one floor of a modest office building in an exurb. She was the only tenant and owned the building and all the property around it for five miles through a convoluted set of corporations and non-profits she funded. Her office was in one corner while the rest of the floor was kept at sixty degrees

Fahrenheit for Miranda, her computers and her bundled-up aide. Titania had balked at bringing in an outsider, even for the most menial jobs, but Miranda weighed three hundred pounds and was gaining every day. Someone had to hose her off occasionally and Titanian simply wasn't up to it. An illegal alien who spoke no English turned out to be the best all around choice.

There was more than the usual computer/air-conditioning hum in Miranda's suite.

"Miranda, are you watching 'Blade Runner' again?" Titania asked, annoyed that she was annoyed.

"It tells me important things about Los Angeles, T," Miranda murmured, not looking up. "I've never been there." Except to type and use the mouse, she didn't move much. She'd never liked loud voices and never used one. Or perhaps her fat muffled it.

"You're always watching 'Blade Runner,'" Titania grumbled.

"It tells me important things about everything."

"I've never thought of it as a documentary or a creed." Titania shook this absurd train of thought off, or at least deferred it for when she had more time to think on it. "Are you really telling me you can't see what's going on in that jail or get either Kate or Helena in there?"

"It is a men's jail, T," Miranda muttered. "With Klaarance in there, DARPA's watching that jail very closely. They are looking for a lead. I would rather not give them one."

"Who's Clarence?"

"It's Klaarance," Miranda said. "Ryan's game name."

"For the love of God, Miranda, call him Ryan," Titania said, rubbing her eyes. "Hasn't he caused enough trouble as Clarence?"

"It's Klaarance. You will be glad to know that Russek is making progress getting Ryan moved to the Twin Towers jail. There will be more opportunity to access him there." Miranda looked up at the only being for whom she would gladly die. "Go fix your make-up, T. You look like a raccoon."

Several jailhouse days went by peacefully, under the circumstances. Bishop had stared down the other three guys in the cell. This was more out of respect for their badassedness than really necessary; if they hadn't tried to kill him for his bunk yet, they weren't going to do so for his punk. They were sensible men sharing that cell, not an ass-rapist among them, and there were prettier items for sale than Drew, so why suffer more than necessary? Bishop's kid was high maintenance anyway, so they steered clear of the situation. Or as clear as five men in an eight-by-twelve foot cell can steer.

For his part, Drew was having trouble adjusting to life in custody. He was embarrassed to use the cell toilet and, even with Bishop keeping an eye on him, he was freaked at showering under the lustful or homicidal gaze of dozens of guys at a time. He was having trouble sleeping spooned up behind Bishop in the narrow bunk to the point of being sleep deprived and his body ached. Moving through the prison was nerve-wracking; he had to stay very close behind Bishop, but not trip on his heels. The one time he lagged too far behind, he'd been groped and badly frightened. Bishop had been right there and punched the guy, but Drew was still creeped out about it. The food was horrible and with nothing but tap water, Drew was slightly dehydrating until Bishop threatened to piss down his throat if he didn't start drinking more water. This might or might not have been an empty threat, so Drew started drinking more water. Drew didn't mention any of this to Russek when he called about getting them moved. Partly because Bishop was standing within earshot, but also because he was starting to like his protector. For all his gruffness and snarl, Bishop was taking very good care of him, and Drew could not fail to appreciate it.

However, taking care of Drew was really starting to wear Bishop out. The jail was full of all kinds of men, some crazy, some just naturally mean and violent, and being mashed together like this wasn't doing anyone's personality disorder any good. Even with his shaved head and dark circles under his eyes, Drew was getting hungry looks, the kind of looks that leave a kid dead after the gang rape. But Bishop kept this to himself; one of the reasons he had Drew keep his eyes down was so he wouldn't see how much danger he was in.

"What'd he say?" Bishop asked when Drew was off the phone.

Drew stared at his shoes. "He's working on it."

"Shit." Bishop led him to a wall and stood a little in front of him. There was no recreation in the jail due to overcrowding; standing around was as good as it got.

Samsa strolled up and said hello. He always seemed to be somewhere lurking in the background. Bishop was still trying to figure out what the cat's game was. If he was after Drew, Bishop pegged him for a guy who would have just asked to make a deal. A few others had made offers and been rebuffed. Bishop wasn't a pimp, or at least not with this kid. This was Russek's kid he was babysitting, and Russek was not a guy to piss off. But Samsa just ignored Drew: noticed him, but then ignored him as he made small talk in response to Bishop's grunts. Eventually Samsa either gave up or saw someone he'd rather talk to. This was always a relief to Bishop; he hated social intercourse.

Undeniably, Bishop was a nicer guy in jail than out of it. The streets were very stressful, you never knew what might come at you or when. At least in jail you knew to always watch your back and there were no surprises, pleasant or otherwise. This gave Bishop a sense of security he'd never had as a free man. He was a solitary sort of person in jail. Minding his own business, he did his time and gave up wanting anything that the State of California and the County of Los Angeles didn't provide. In other lock-ups he had allowed himself a very small circle of thugs he dug to stand around with in the yard. And hookers when he

33

could afford it. But never ever, ever, ever a punk. He'd seen some nice prison marriages, but even those well-behaved punks seemed like too much hassle, too many guys to fight off, too much territory to defend, and even a kind of future for two to worry about, even if the future was only until parole. Or death. Toss into the mix having to provide for more than his own needs, and the sex and housekeeping hardly seemed worth it to Bishop. And now look at him, just look at him, he was in the same stupid husband-like situation with a punk he couldn't even get off with. Life was against him, always against him, always grinding him down, ruining his day, even in jail, where he was usually at least minimally content.

The bell rang for dinner. Bishop shook himself and watched the crowd heading for the mess hall. He glanced at Drew, who was watching him. "Hey, shut up, just shut the mutherfuck up," he snarled and walked off, Drew close behind him.

The next day, when most of the guards were occupied with a minor riot in another part of the complex, five guys grabbed Drew in the rush after lunch and dragged him under a stairwell. Bishop had seen it coming, he just couldn't do anything about it. Although Drew put up as much fight as he had in him—which was negligible to embarrassing by jailhouse standards—five guys—or four and a half if the one struggling with Drew was factored in—were just too much for even a motherfucker like Bishop. So this was the first time Bishop was almost glad to see Samsa come smashing into the mix.

Samsa wasn't a great fighter, but an effective one. He kicked the shit out of the guy holding Drew, who was trying to drag the kid away. Punching his way past one thug, Samsa kept Drew behind him, while scaring off another. That left the two who were wearing Bishop down. One of them pulled a shiv and cut Samsa's bicep before Samsa broke his arm and the one fighting Bishop wisely fled.

Stunned but still on his feet, Bishop leaned on Drew as they followed Samsa back to his cell, which was closest. No one was there and by then Bishop's battered head had cleared. "Hey, thanks, man, we must be going," he said.

"That looks pretty bad," Drew said, gently lifting Samsa's bloody sleeve away from the knife gash.

"Don't talk to him!" Bishop snarled, and then looked at Samsa's arm. "That looks bad," he agreed and then turned to Drew. "Find something to fix it up, kid, but don't talk to him."

Samsa gestured to the sink with his head. "Just a scratch," he said.

"Then let's go, kid." Bishop was all business again and wanting to be out of there before the inevitable request got requested.

"Yeah, a scratch I got helping ya out," Samsa said. "I think ya owe me a little somethin' for that."

"Shit," Bishop thought, but said, "He fixing your arm up." He watched as Drew sat on the bunk with Samsa and rather efficiently cleaned the wound with soap and water, then wrapped a t-shirt around it.

"It's not my arm needs fixing," Samsa said, staring hard at Drew's mouth.

"What you want, Samsa?" Bishop finally asked, just to get it over with.

"A kiss."

"I don't kiss guys."

"From him."

Drew had his eyes down, his expression unreadable. Bishop mentally shrugged and walked over to the bunk. Samsa defensively got up. "Open your mouth," Bishop ordered, and peered inside when Samsa complied. "Okay, but no tongue," he said when he'd satisfied himself that Samsa didn't have any open sores or other disgusting things in his mouth. "Just do it, Drew," Bishop said, looking up and down the crowded tier. He angled his body to hide the two men on the bunk.

"Drew," Samsa said gently. "Your name's Drew, huh?" The kid nodded without looking up. "I'm not gonna hurt ya."

"Hurry up," Bishop said, hoping the guys coming down the tier weren't heading for the cell.

Samsa slipped his uninjured arm around Drew's waist and pulled him into a chaste, but electric, kiss. Bishop frowned as Drew arched against the other man and let his eyes fall shut, his way-too-long-for-a-guy lashes brushing his cheek. "A hug's not part of this deal," Bishop growled. Samsa removed his arm, but neither of them moved back. "Hey, are you done yet?" Bishop asked sarcastically.

At some signal between the men, Drew opened his eyes and leaned back. "Thank you for helping me," he said softly, eyes lowered.

"Shut up. He was helping me," Bishop said in a deadly low voice. "Let's go, kid."

"Yeah, Drew, I was only helping Bishop," Samsa said, watching Drew stand up and walk over to his protector. "And, you're fucking welcome, Bishop, thanks for everything."

"Fuck you, Samsa, we even." Bishop roughly grabbed Drew and shoved him out of the cell in front of him. At the end of the tier, he pressed Drew against the wall to let a swarm of men pass them and hissed, "Don't ever kiss anyone like that in the jailhouse," into the frightened kid's ear. Bishop shoved his groin against Drew's semi-hard-on, which immediately shriveled, to underscore his message. He hardly spoke to him for two days after that. Drew, of course, kept his mouth shut and eyes down.

After a good night's sleep and a hard look at all the hard looks Drew was getting, especially from the injured guys from the day before, Bishop easily made a hard decision. Finding a way to make it sound like he was doing Samsa a huge favor and not even hinting that he needed help keeping Drew safe, Bishop cut a deal to give Samsa limited and heavily supervised access to

Drew. Ignoring Drew's panicky look, he negotiated the bastard down from ass-fucking access to hand jobs and closed-mouth kisses access.

"And conversation," Samsa added, glancing at the somewhat alarmed Drew over Bishop's shoulder. "I get to talk to him and give him presents."

"Hey, am I running a fucking escort service here?" Bishop asked acidly.

"Ya doing me a favor here, Bishop," Samsa said with a devil-may-care shrug. "I'm just asking."

"Fuck." Sighing dramatically, Bishop escorted the pair to Samsa's empty cell, where Drew clumsily jerked him off. So clumsily, Samsa had to reach down and help him out. It was embarrassing how unskilled at masturbating another guy the kid was. Bishop wondered just how much Russek was getting out of him. Calmly watching the tier as the two men fumbled their way to Samsa's orgasm, Bishop thanked his cruel God that Samsa didn't drag it out. At least Drew was less aroused after this encounter; he kept his eyes open and didn't lean into it when Samsa kissed him good-bye, so Bishop had nothing to scold him about afterwards.

Having Samsa watching Drew's back made Bishop's life a little easier until they were moved to the Twin Towers a few days later. Then Bishop's life was much easier when he and Drew were in a two-man cell all by themselves.

Chapter 4

A Policeman's Lot

The Department Manager scratched his chin and consulted his notes. "How did the DHS and FBI make the Russek connection so quickly?" he asked the Section Manager.

"I'm not really sure," the Section Manager said.

This always annoyed Titania because it meant he could defer his answer, his responsibility, and even reality indefinitely. The only thing worse was when he deferred a question to Titania's superior knowledge, completely letting him off the hook.

"Titania knows more about the nuts and bolts of this than I do," he said.

"You worm," she thought, but kept her face placid and professional as she said, "Williams sends up red flags on most of the security networks worldwide. The only people not keeping track of him are whoever thinks they have him on a leash. Russek's statement went into the LAPD database, which feeds into the FBI and DHS databases, and that's how they knew Williams was in, or had recently been, in Los Angeles with Russek. However, even I was a little surprised at how fast Agents Romero and Carpenter got to Russek in LA."

"And why is that?" the Section Manager sneered. "Don't you have access to the same information as the DHS and the FBI?"

"Of course," she said, cool as a lily. "I was merely surprised that Russek knew Williams as Williams. He only uses his real name with people he respects, and this made Russek a very dangerous person."

"Oh, bugger." Kate turned the volume up a little on her

headphones

Helena and Isabella looked away from their laptops and waited.

"Romero and Carpenter just went into Russek's place," Kate said "You'd better ring up Titania."

"I'm fixin' to." Helena logged into a porn site to send Titania a coded message to call her.

"I thought DHS and the FBI weren't speaking," Isabella said, innocently rolling her hazel eyes. She would know; she'd planted enough evidence and hooked enough of their agents on her online gaming scams to make each of them think the other was the anti-Christ, if not the devil himself.

"All is forgiven where Williams is concerned," Helena said. She dug out her cell phone. She didn't trust the landline of the house they'd broken into. They'd have to move fairly soon; the former residents' bodies were starting to stink. "What are they talking about?" she asked Isabella, who'd put on headphones and jacked into what Kate was listening to.

"Just introductions so far," Isabella said. "Oh, lawdy..."

"What!?" Helena hissed.

"They're sweeping for bugs."

"I wired the neighbors," Helena said, bringing up her plastics page. "A nice little explosion should distract them. There."

"Nothing," Isabella said, trying to adjust the static out of her headphones as the sweep closed in. "What did you wire? The house or the car?"

"The car."

"Well, darlin', that could be anywhere," Isabella observed.

"Hang on," Kate said. "The bugs are up the spout. We'll have to wire it up again when they leave."

"Where the fuck did those come from?" Russek snarled at the bugs in Agent Romero's hand.

"Hard to say, Detective Russek, hard to say," Agent

Carpenter drawled as Romero pocketed the devices. "Now do you see why we came all the way out here from D.C. to chat with you in person."

"Yeah, damn." Russek invited them to sit down and even got out some sun tea for them.

"All clear," Carpenter said, coming back from one last sweep.

"Find anything else?" Romero asked as he poured sugar into his tea. He was a compact Black man and his movements were smooth and graceful.

"Nah, nice clean job." Carpenter opened his briefcase and carefully put his equipment away. He drew a folder out and handed Russek a photograph. "We'd like to discuss this man with you."

Russek stared at the photo of himself in dusty fatigues and a tall and lean man with salt and pepper hair, a chiseled profile, and an immaculate black uniform. The photo was taken too far away to see the other man's dark blue eyes and his smile wasn't his usual devilish grin. Just looking at him, Russek could almost hear his infectious laugh. He looked at the photo's blank backside, turned it over and stared a little more. "Am I going to need a lawyer?" he asked. "Because this man saved my life in Kabul."

"We know," Romero said with a friendly smile. "And we know you know that that photo was taken about fifteen minutes before you were attacked by a terrorist. That photo was taken by the CIA; they were keeping an eye on Williams."

"Why?" Russek asked and got blank stares. "I mean, why were they keeping an eye—"

"Oh...should I tell him or do you want to?" Romero asked Carpenter.

"Go 'head, you're a better raconteur than I am." Carpenter sat back to study Russek with his Nordic blue eyes. Tall and thin, he let Romero do the talking whenever they got stuck on the same bad job together.

They were anti-terrorism experts and if things went very wrong, they were clean-up men. Technically, they weren't authorized to kill, but they were authorized to disappear subjects or at least make it look like an accident.

"This man you know as Warren Williams goes by many names, depending on who he's working for at the moment," Romero said. "We thought he was working for Army Intelligence in Kabul, but the CIA thought he was working for them. It seems now he was either freelancing for MI6 or on his own errand there. We really don't know. He did collect paychecks from both the Army and Langley—Langley accounting noticed the double dip when they hacked into the Army's pay records, that's when the CIA decided to see what he was really up to—but we still have no idea what he was there for. What did he tell you?"

"He was wearing a Blackwater uniform," Russek said. "I didn't ask any questions."

"Blackwater is in so many hotspots," Romero said. "The CIA, what's left of the KGB and the good Lord knows who else have been sliding in and out of secure areas in those uniforms for years now. Did he say anything else?"

"No," Russek said. "You might or might not know this, but I only met him that morning. I was trying to buy some decent food—that slop the Army buys from KBR is vile—and I was having language problems. Warren helped me out. Hell, he bought us both breakfast and ate with me. He's a very friendly guy."

"That's what they tell me, very nice, very charming," Romero said. "What did you two talk about?"

"This and that," Russek said. "Mainly about what a fucked-up mess the world was because of the United States and how much we wanted to be home. He said he was from Savannah, said he missed the sea."

"That's new," Carpenter said, making a note on his file folder. "He usually tells people he's from Madison, Wisconsin."

"Is he?" Russek asked.

"No one know where Williams is from," Romero said. "Or even what his real name is." He glanced at his watch. "So, based on one breakfast and one ambush, Williams decided to visit you here in Los Angeles. Didn't that seem odd to you?"

"No," Russek said. "I gave him my LAPD card, told him if he ever wanted to visit LA, go to Disneyland, Hollywood, wherever, to look me up. Like I said, he was a very nice guy. And he saved my life. It was the least I could do."

"And when he got here, you lent him your car," Romero said, consulting his nonexistent notes. "Why did you follow him if he was such a nice guy?"

"Because that particular industrial park in the middle of the night isn't Disneyland or Hollywood Boulevard," Russek said. "I thought it was very strange that he was down there. I also thought someone might have stolen my car from him—that happens in LA sometimes—so I went to have a look."

"Taking the police with you?" Romero asked.

"It's a tough neighborhood," Russek said. "Turned out to be a tough situation." He sighed. "And, like you said, I didn't know him so well. He was Blackwater, too. If he'd been Army or Marines...it's not that Blackwater ops are bad people, but they're in it for the money, not serving their country."

"I disagree with you, Detective," Carpenter said. "Blackwater ops are mercenary motherfuckers who have no honor or decency and should be gunned down on sight by anyone and everyone. But Williams is worse; he's a terrorist mercenary motherfucker and we've been after him for years."

"If I'd known that," Russek said slowly. "I would've called you when he called me from the airport." He let that sink in. "So who bugged my apartment?"

"Could be anyone," Carpenter said, holding up the bugs. "We use these, but so does anyone who takes pride in their surveillance work."

"I see," Russek said blandly. "More tea for you guys?" he asked.

"No, thank you," Romero said, gathering up his briefcase. "We'll be in touch if we have more questions."

"You know where to find me," Russek said. "Did you want this back?" He held out the photo of him and Williams on the Kabul street.

"You can keep that," Romero said. He and Carpenter said their goodbyes and left.

After seeing them out, Russek leaned the photo on the mantle with their cards. He looked at the photo for a minute, and then put it and the cards face down. Russek had been a cop for fifteen years by then and he knew when people were lying to him. Carpenter and Romero were lying when they said they didn't know who bugged his place. He didn't think they were lying about anything else, but they were definitely holding something back.

When he got to Parker Center for his shift, Russek did two things: the first was to run Romero and Carpenter through the Police databases. They appeared to be who they said they were, but there wasn't a lot of detail on them. Then Russek asked the LAPD electronics wizards to quietly sweep his house and leave anything they found. They found a new set of bugs. They said, just on visual inspection, they were high quality equipment of the type used by top-notch crime fighting organizations like the FBI, the CIA, and, well, the LAPD.

"Who's after you, Paul?" his captain asked when Russek ran it down for him.

"I don't think it's me so much as the company I keep."

"Damn," Titania said over the secure line she ran through the Harvard Divinity School. "But the good news is Miranda hacked the equipment those idiots left behind. We'll hear what they're hearing, but it's better than being completely shut out. Russek also logged on and ran checks on what there is about those two fools. He must be suspicious."

"He's a policeman, Titania," Kate said. "They're naturally suspicious." She'd pulled over in Westwood to take Titania's call, so she was sitting in the Cadillac Escalade she'd jacked in Beverly Hills. Few people feel threatened when a well-dressed middle-aged woman asks for help finding her car. Mostly they feel annoyed or amused until they feel dead and stuffed in their own trunk. "You certainly took your time calling us back."

"I was having a rather stressful chat with our patron over at Observatory Circle, trying to explain why the Los Angeles situation only looks like it's coming apart at the seams." Titania's voice was calm, as usual, but sounded very, very tired. "The details are under control, and you know the devil is in the details, but the big picture is really too big to tell how much the details are under control."

"Oh, the bloody details are under control, but we're stuck, we're stalled, we're not moving forward, and it could go pear-shaped any minute," Kate said, annoyed that Titania was spinning her the same tale she'd spun for that madman in charge. "The details and everything else is frozen solid until we can get what we need out of Ryan."

"Yes, dear, I know. That was the other reason I was so late in calling you back: I was arguing with Viola. She doesn't want to come help you out," Titania said with disarming candor.

"Then we don't need her," Kate snapped. "We're perfectly capa–"

"I know, I'll leave the rough stuff in your perfectly capable hands," Titania said briskly. "But Viola will have influence with Ryan that you don't. After all, you weren't his lover in Baku."

"I don't shag anyone that young," Kate said, loftily. "But I see your point."

"Not to worry, my dear, better days are coming,"

Titania said, winding down. "We've got Helena in the Twin Towers starting tomorrow. She might be able to get the information we need out of Ryan and you can all get the hell out of Los Angeles."

"Sooner done, sooner gone."

"Amen to that," Titania said. "Oh, and Kate; if Russek's visitors are in town, that means they might have their own people on the ground, snooping around. The LAPD isn't as dumb as it looks either. You three will have to stir the water to keep them all off balance until we're done with Ryan."

"Understood. We're low on C4 and weapons. Can you get some to us?" Kate asked, and ran down the list she, Helena and Isabella had put together the night before. "How will you get it to us?"

"I'll have it delivered to the Secure Borders Project's Los Angeles arms depot. You'll have to steal it from there," Titania said. "I'll have Miranda send you all the details you'll need. She's been cultivating them online because they're crazy enough to be useful someday. We'll make it look like the supplies are coming from the Klan or some other sympathetic racist group. We'll tell them there's a Black and Brown insurgency brewing or something equally ridiculous."

"They sound like a bunch of daft buggers," Kate said

"Perhaps. But they're useful 'daft buggers' for us."

"By the way, Titania, how do you know Ryan's stolen data hasn't blown us already?" Kate asked, eyeing her next vehicle: a silver Mercedes S class.

"Because we're all still alive to worry about it."

Chapter 5

Detention Doldrums

Titania took off her jacket, draped it neatly over her chair-back, and adjusted her cuffs. She wasn't sure if the Section Manager and the Department Manager were looking at her shoulder holster or her breasts, and had no time to verify it because they looked away when she got settled. "Due to Romero and Carpenter's arrival in Los Angeles, our operatives on the ground were occupied with small and random acts of civil disruption to keep the DHS, FBI and LAPD too busy to track us down," Titania said blandly. She was conserving her strength for evasions yet to come.

"Yes. I've read of few of the police reports from those weeks," her Section Manager snarled. He was sweating; it was unattractive. "You and your people drove an entire urban center into a frenzy and a collective nervous breakdown."

"Yes," Titania said. "We did. We needed the time with Ryan." She cleared her throat and sipped a little tepid coffee. "Once Ryan was moved to the Twin Towers Jail, we were able to get an operative in contact with him," she continued. "Our operative had to be gentle so he didn't get spooked. He's a very high-strung young man."

"How did you get your operative inside the jail?" the Department Manager asked.

"As the replacement for the usual jail psychologist," she answered.

"And this aroused no suspicions on the part of the Los Angeles Sheriff's Department?" her Section Manager asked.

"No, no more than a cursory glance," she said.

"The jails were so full of suspected terrorists, the Sheriffs were so overwhelmed with emergencies and screw-ups—bad ones—they could barely deal with the basic jail bureaucracy. Something as mundane and conflict-free as a replacement psychologist was barely a ripple in their system."

"I also read the police reports for those weeks, Agent Titania," the Department Manager said without much inflection. "What did you and your operation get out of all of it?"

Titania folded her hands in her lap and smiled like a banker about to deny a loan. "I would have to say we got...mixed results."

Ryan's first night in his own bunk (the upper, of course) in the Twin Towers passed without incident. The next day, after a look around with Bishop, caused him to realize two things: the first was that, yes, they had their own cell, but second, the cellblock they were in was full of scarier men than the Men's Jail. He asked Bishop about this after lunch.

"This is where they put the violent criminoid mutherfuckers," Bishop said blandly. He was watching the hallway crowds; a few eyed Drew, but they were merely noticed and then ignored. "There were a lot of suspected terrorists like you, in the Men's Jail. There were violent criminoid mutherfuckers over there, but they were working off their excess energy on the suspected terrorists, like you, but unlike you, the suspected terrorists who didn't have a violent criminoid mutherfucker bodyguard, like me. We got the same problem here, just a different, more focused, kind of tension."

"Are they...? Do they...? Um...will they...?"

"Rape you?" Bishop watched Drew nod. "Yeah, most of 'em, if they got the chance." He let that sink in as Drew paled even a little more. "Missing your boyfriend Samsa?"

"No," Drew lied. "Are you?"

48

"Yeah. I am."

That night, Drew had a nightmare and an asthma attack.

At first Bishop was annoyed that Drew, for whatever reason, woke him up. His irritation changed into alarm when he heard Drew's rasping wheezing and watched his panicky scrabbling for the inhaler. "Fuck, Drew. Are you okay?" he asked, pulling the shaking kid into his arms.

Still working on the inhaler, Drew nodded and trustingly laid his head on Bishop's muscular shoulder. "I'm hokay," he said when he could draw enough breath. "Had a nightmare."

"Nightmares give you asthma?" Bishop asked. It sounded stupid to him when he heard it come out of his mouth, but there was no going back now.

"Sometimes."

"Shit." Bishop tightened his arms a little around Drew, who seemed to be falling asleep on his feet. "Gimme that thing," he said, taking the inhaler from the kid. He put it under his pillow and pulled Drew into the bunk with him. "You sleep with me tonight," he said, turning Drew to face the cell and spooning up behind him. "I want you and that thing right here if you have another nightmare."

Too sleepy to resist, Drew shifted around to get comfortable, pulled Bishop's arm over him like a security blanket, and went to sleep.

Bishop's penultimate thought before sleep was along the lines of how neatly Drew fit into his arms. His last thought was how much Russek owed him for being such a fucking saint to look after this kid.

There are a few moments every jailhouse morning, before the wake-up bell rings, when a man can assess his failures, resign himself to his fate, and drag himself into another day. But Bishop was having difficulty working up the appropriate jailbird forbearance with his morning wood snuggled between Drew's thighs as the kid peacefully went on sleeping.

Bishop didn't consider himself an opportunist, but he wasn't stupid either. The confined routine of jail flat-lined his aggression and had a similar effect on his libido. He liked sex, but he liked sex on his terms, not the kind of sex two men could have when the Sheriffs were distracted elsewhere. He also liked sex in bigger beds and, preferably, in the middle of the afternoon. And with girls, if they were really pretty (and even if they weren't). But he was already three-quarters of the way to an orgasm when he eased his cock out of his county-issue shorts and began to move it between Drew's soft thighs. His hand was poised over Drew's mouth to cut off any protest, so Bishop was a little surprised when instead of struggling, Drew began to move with him. Sliding his hand down Drew's chest, over his hard nipples and taut belly, Bishop eased the kid's leaking erection out of his underwear and stroked him in time to his intercrural rhythm. Bishop put his hand over Drew's mouth when they came: the kid was noisy.

They were both breathing a little harder than usual, but after a happy little sigh, Drew dozed off. Bishop wasn't sure the kid had ever completely woken up, but didn't care because he was dozing off himself. Not long afterwards, the morning bell jolted them and several hundred other inmates awake. Neither Drew nor Bishop mentioned a stickiness in certain intimate places. Although Bishop noticed Drew seemed a little more relaxed and secure that day, he never asked the kid why.

"Maybe I dreamed it," Bishop thought, while he waited for Drew to finish his meeting with Dr. Smith. "Maybe I need my head examined, too."

Inside the office used for inmate psychological counseling, Helena looked disgustedly at the metal desk, plastic chairs, and scuffed-up linoleum. She'd been in classier jails than this one, jails with real character: iron bars, exposed brick, and concrete floors. This was way too much like Social Services or the Housing Authority.

There was a panic button on the desk, but that gave her little comfort since she figured she could handle any rough stuff better than the flabby deputies she'd seen on her way in.

This Ryan kid was no prize either. Since he'd sat down, he hadn't been able to make eye contact with her or answer in more than monosyllables. That was fine; gave her a chance to study on him a little. She hadn't quite found the trigger to get him talking. Of course she couldn't pry too hard; the session was being monitored, just in case the inmate attacked her.

"So, Andrew— You mind if I call you Andrew?" she asked.

"No."

"Andrew, are you feeling stressed?" Helena twirled her pencil and stared at the top of Ryan's head.

"Now?"

"Yes, and in general." If only she could stare a hole into it and get what she needed out of it.

"Yes."

"Why is that?"

Ryan looked up and quickly looked away. "I'm in jail."

"But is that fear or stress?" More pencil twirling.

"I dunno."

"I'll tell ya why I ask." She slammed the pencil on the desk and he jumped. "There's a difference between fear and stress, even though they can feel the same. But fear is useless whereas stress, channeled properly, is useful and constructive. Are you with me so far?"

He shook his shaved head.

"Fear is irrational, therefore useless; it forces us to do things based on our animal nature, to react from our lizard brain," Helena said patiently. She adjusted her faux tortoise shell glasses and pushed a lock of tawny brown wig hair off her taupe cashmere-clad shoulder. Dr. Smith, as impersonated by Helena, was a study in shades of brown. "But stress can be beneficial. Stress presses on us just enough to either bring out our best or bring out our worst. How are you handling the stresses and challenges of being in jail, Andrew?"

"...Okay."

"Making any new friends in here?"

"No."

"Been gang-raped yet?"

"No!" He looked up at her.

"Would you like to be?" She held his gaze.

"No."

"No what?"

"No, ma'am." He looked away.

Ryan's file was annoyingly thin. Helena would have to get Miranda to put more in it for her to work with. She couldn't bring up Baku because there was no mention of it. Ryan had given Russek's home address as his; as far as the Sheriffs were concerned, Ryan had been born there. She glanced at the institutional wall clock; they still had some time left on their fifty minute hour. "Tell me a happy memory," she prompted.

"Um...I dunno."

"Ah. Well. What's your favorite ice cream flavor?" she asked.

"Vanilla."

"Really. Hm."

After Ryan left, Helena spent the next few hours listening to several inmates' sick sexual fantasies, one perfectly understandable suicidal rant, and a pack of charming lies masquerading as compliments by an inmate trying to pick her up. She recommended anti-psychotics for all of them, especially the guy who thought he was in a pick-up bar instead of the County lock-up, and scheduled another session with Ryan the next day. Or tried to: as it turned out, her headshrinking schedule was jam packed with assorted recidivist nutcases, so the best she could do was get Ryan again in two days.

After passing through Dr. Smith's anteroom, and being violently eyed by several huge men there, Drew was greatly relieved to see Bishop waiting for him in the hall.

"How was it?" Bishop asked.

"She wanted to know what kind of ice cream I like."

"What?"

"Vanilla," Drew said. "I like vanilla ice cream."

"Is that...is that why you need counseling?" Bishop asked, looking around the too deserted hallway.

"I don't know, I...um..." Drew stopped talking and moved closer to Bishop. He'd picked up Bishop's sudden wariness a little too late.

They rounded a corner and were faced by four very big, very hard-looking men. Bishop began to retreat the way they'd come, but two more men cut off that avenue of escape. Bishop was not a coward, but he had doubts about his chances in this fight. He suspected Drew was better at running than fighting. He also knew he didn't have a chance against six men. He put his body between Drew and the men. Drew's back was against the wall. Bishop dearly hoped Drew would run back the way they'd come and get help when he punched a hole in the two guys blocking that route. "I'm sure this is just a misunderstanding," he growled.

"Bishop, I got no mess with you," the supposed lead rapist said. "This will only take twenty, maybe thirty minutes, and you can watch."

Bishop felt Drew gasp and stiffen behind him and prayed the kid wouldn't faint. Even though Bishop thought passing out and waking up might be the best thing in this situation if–

"Yeah, I wanna watch, too," a familiar scary voice said from the back of the larger group of rapists. "I wanna watch ya mutherfuckers eat yer teeth!"

While Samsa kidney-punched his way through the back of the pack, Bishop smashed his fist into the nearest inmate and kicked the one next nearest in the nuts. They both went down like sacks of potatoes. With the main group occupied with Samsa, Bishop saw his opening, grabbed Drew and ran for it.

"Wait!" Drew said, looking back at Samsa still fighting.

"He'll find us!" Bishop slung the kid over his shoulder and ran down the hall with him. He heard a few more wet crunches behind him and then running feet. Just one pair, and since Drew wasn't freaking out, he figured it was Samsa.

Bishop put Drew down when they got closer to a more populated area, but kept going towards their cell. Drew was white as a sheet and Bishop had bruised knuckles, but Samsa had a bloody nose and was bleeding from the corner of his mouth.

A deputy stopped them. "What the fuck happened to you?" he asked Samsa.

"I ran into a cell door," Samsa said lamely, his fat lip slurring his words a little.

The deputy looked dubious until Drew piped up. "We're going to fix him up, Officer," the kid said respectfully.

The deputy knew Bishop by sight and looked a question at him. "Yeah. We are," Bishop said with the requisite combination of jailhouse resignation and irony, maybe too much.

"You don't sound very happy about it, Bishop," the deputy observed.

"I hate clumsy people," Bishop said blandly.

"Oh." The deputy gave them one last look and let them go.

When they got to their cell, Bishop shoved Drew into the wall and got right in his face. "Eyes down, mouth shut," he said in a murderous voice.

"S...sorry," Drew whispered and carefully edged past him to the sink where he ran cold water on a towel to clean up Samsa's face.

After one look at Bishop's furious face, Samsa took the towel and cleaned himself up. "I overhead them guys talkin' 'bout it," he said, checking his hatchet face in the tiny mirror over the sink. "I just got here, but they said yer name, Bishop, so I knew who they were talking; about and what they were gonna do. I didn't know where the counseling center was or I woulda come to warn you, so I followed them." Samsa glanced at Drew, whose eyes were demurely lowered, and then at Bishop, who was scowling at Drew. "So...here I am."

Barely moving his head, Bishop shifted his glare to him. "What you want, Samsa?"

"Same deal I had before," Samsa said blandly.

"Fuck!" Bishop spat.

"Can I get that, too?" Samsa asked.

"You're a fucking laugh riot," Bishop said less lethally. "All right. I got the same problem, so you got the same deal. Drew! Get on with it! Don't make a mess." Bishop turned away to watch the tier so he didn't have to see Drew's clumsy handjob technique.

Behind him Samsa sat on the bunk next to Drew. "Listen, ya like this kind of gum?" he asked, handing the kid a package of Trident original flavor.

"I do, thanks," Drew said, taking a stick and handing the package back.

"No, it's all for you," Samsa said. He glanced at Bishop, who'd made a groan-like noise and tapped his head against the bars. "Um, listen, Drew, I don't think I can get it up, not even for you, so maybe we could just talk. Yeah?" Drew nodded, and looked up at him from under lowered lashes. Samsa thought, "That's a fucking dangerous look, baby," but asked, "So, what did you do today?"

"I saw a psychologist named Dr. Smith," he said. "She–"

"She? What'd she look like?" Samsa ignored Bishop, who'd turned to look at him.

"She, um, I didn't look too closely," Drew said. "She was old, had brown hair and wore glasses..."

"No scars on her face? On the left side? And missing an eye?" Samsa asked. He could almost feel Bishop's glare burning a hole in him.

"No, nothing like that," Drew said, sounding

scandalized. "I would have remembered something like that. She wanted to know what kind of ice cream I liked."

"She...did?" Samsa asked, nonplussed.

"Yeah, I like vanilla," Drew said, glancing between the two men staring at him.

"Really."

"Your time's up, Samsa," Bishop said. He sounded very tired.

Samsa stood up with Drew. He tilted Drew's chin up and gave him a light kiss. "My mouth hurts," he said. "I'll give ya a better kiss next time."

"Your nose is swelling up, too," the kid observed and then looked at the floor.

"Get. Out." Bishop moved between the two men, but didn't touch either of them.

"See ya tomorrow," Samsa said pleasantly and went on his way.

Bishop stood in the middle of the cell watching Drew tidying up after Samsa's visit. "I really hate your boyfriend," he finally said.

"Oh?"

"But I'm really fucking glad he showed up when he did." Bishop turned his back and ignored Drew until dinner time. And continued to ignore him after dinner, right up until he pulled Drew into his bunk on the pretext of needing to be close in case of nightmares and asthma attacks. Bishop was only lying to Drew; he knew perfectly well he was looking forward to having the same dream with Drew in the morning.

"What do you think the best way to get the ammo from the Secure Border Project is?" Kate asked Helena and Isabella from the driver's seat. "Should we hijack the lorry—"

"The whut?" Helena asked, looking at her from the passenger seat.

"Sorry, hijack the truck before it gets to their safe house or take it from the safe house after they unload it?" They were on the Pasadena Freeway heading for downtown to pick up some money at one of Miranda's ATMs. They'd been wearing various wigs and sunglasses all morning, roaming from one ATM to another all over the city to get enough cash to keep going. Not that they needed much cash, but it was good to have. Breaking into wealthy homes, killing everyone they found there, and stealing whatever they needed not only gave them nice places to sleep, but kept them in good shape for clothes, cars and cash. Kate was wearing a Chanel suit and driving a Jaguar from their last home invasion.

"I say we grab the truck—"

"Or lorry," Isabella put in from the back seat.

"Hush, sugar, I say we grab it before it gets to their safe house," Helena said. She was wearing an Escada pantsuit that was a little too small for her, but the Tiffany wristwatch fit just fine. "But there's only three of us, Kate, and we all got bad backs so loading it up and unloading isn't such a great idea."

"Wellll, but we don't have a good place to hide it," Isabella said. She'd mostly ignored the clothes and jewelry, only allowing Helena to force some new shoes and a lightweight jacket on her.

"We can park it on the street and just keep moving it," Helena suggested.

"We did that in San Francisco once and the damn thing got impounded," Kate said, omitting the "I told you so," that usually accompanied this story.

"Where's their safe house?" Isabella asked. Kate gave her an address in El Segundo. "Why don't we take the drop after the shipment is unloaded? How big is this Secure Borders Project operation? We could say we were there for a special mission."

"Not a bad idea," Kate said.

"Let's talk to Titania first," Helena said. "She might have a better idea."

"She does sometimes," Isabella agreed.

"Bugger!" Kate hissed. "That little bint in the Honda

won't let me merge over! Somebody shoot her."

"There's a child in a car seat in the back," Isabella observed laconically. She was deciding between the Walther or the UZI pistol. She was like the surfeited swain with guns, who could be happy with either, t'were the other dear charmer away. She decided on the UZI.

"Oh, well, then," Kate said, pulling slightly ahead as she missed her turn-off. "Just shoot out a tyre."

Every morning since the asthma attack, Drew woke up with Bishop gently jacking him off. He stayed very still because Bishop stopped if Drew seemed to be awake. And Drew very much didn't want Bishop to stop. He was in a bizarre situation, but his sex drive was normal for a man his age. If Bishop wanted to jack him off while getting off between his legs, that was fine, maybe even better than fine, with Drew, if only for the novelty of it. The problem would be if Bishop wanted more because Drew wasn't sure he'd say no, even though he was in love with Russek. In his admittedly limited experience, he'd never felt the way he felt about Russek before. He thought he was in love with John, but John left him high and dry in the DARPA building where Paul saved him. He'd also read enough porn to know the difference between love and lust. So he was sure he loved Paul, but he was turned on by John, the mysterious Mademoiselle in Baku, Bishop, and Samsa.

Of course the only one Drew was getting any sexual release from was Bishop when they were technically asleep. Although he was still spending closely monitored by Bishop time with Samsa in exchange for the bodyguard back-up, Samsa was less interested in the hand-job, and more interested conversation. Specifically hearing about where Drew had lived and what he'd done in his short life. Bishop thought it was odd, but although Drew didn't say anything, he was really enjoying Samsa's good-bye kiss. He liked kissing, and he missed it very much.

Outside the jail there were mysterious car accidents, murders, fires and explosions keeping the city on edge and the cops fully occupied.

Isabella and Helena worked well as a team. One of their favorite plays was for one of them to be in the biggest stolen car they could find, crash it across a busy freeway at rush hour and be picked up and whisked away by the other on a motorcycle. Singly, they could do a lot of damage with a handgun on a motorcycle at rush hour as well. Or not at rush hour, when one shot could spin a car out of control and cause a major pile up. The problem then was that other cars might chase them and try to run them down. Or shoot at them. This was when grenades were especially handy. Because they couldn't be everywhere at once, they mined a few of the busier freeways and left C4 on timers in some of the more traveled surface streets.

Other drivers were helping destabilize the city as well. Random freeway shootings went up and stayed up. As was usual, people drove better after a few shootings, but the frequency didn't decrease, although drivers and driving in Los Angeles and surrounding areas continued to improve. Miranda, following events on the internet (news and blogs), speculated that this was due to sympathetic magical thinking, in that there was really nothing, aside from barricading themselves in their homes, drivers could do to avoid being shot other than being a good driver, which meant going with the flow of traffic and not attracting attention to themselves, and hoping for the best. Fearful times and capricious fate had spawned a new kind of secular/vehicular religion that Miranda, who didn't drive, go outside, or believe in an interventionist God, didn't entirely disapprove of.

Isabella was intrigued by the nightlife on Hollywood Boulevard and after an hour of looking at it, stole a semitruck and crashed along the curb, knocking cars hither and thither on the north side of it. She took out block after block, smashing up the sidewalks and storefronts on stretches where there weren't telephone poles. Helena picked her up on a motorcycle when another truck crashed into Isabella's vehicle in an intersection.

"I'm not so sure this was a good idea," Helena grumbled under the sirens getting closer from all directions. She picked up her Heckler und Koch submachine gun with a silencer and started shooting the traffic trying to get around the accident.

Isabella threw a grenade into the cab of the truck and shot up her own share of traffic. They didn't flee the scene until someone took a shot at them. "How dare they shoot at us," she said when they were out of danger.

"This is El Lay, honey, these people only seem like wimps," Helena said, pulling into a parking garage to steal a new vehicle. "They're willing live here with earthquakes, wildfires and riots. They act like everything is great, but you push 'em hard enough and some of them will fuck you up. Smiling and friendly-like while they do, too."

"What time is it?" Isabella asked after mulling that over for a moment.

"Nearly midnight."

"Let's do the other side of the street from the other direction," Isabella said reasonably. "The cops should be gone in an hour and no one will be expecting it."

It was so insane, no one was expecting it. Just to add a little variation, Isabella threw grenades out the window as she crashed down the south side of Hollywood Boulevard. The city was no more ready for that than they had been for the earlier attack. But after that, the city, if not the LAPD, knew they were attacks, not random insane acts of deranged but highly organized, mysterious and elusive persons.

Kate had a different style of urban terrorism. She looked so pleasant and harmless, normally cautious citizens let down their guard enough for her to kill them and proceed from there. If they were interesting enough men or women, she'd often allow them to buy her meals, have fascinating conversations, sometimes sex of varying quality, and then she'd kill them and proceed from there.

In addition to home invasion, murder, and theft, her procedures for Los Angeles were small scale arson and car bombs. After breaking into or being ushered into her target, she'd plant a small amount of explosive in a highly flammable area and set a timer for it. The building's sprinklers would stop the fire from spreading, but the fire alarm would bring a swarm of firetrucks, sirens blaring, and this was her intent. Kate was not there to clear city blocks, although she easily could with enough C4: she was there to panic the locals. Nothing inspires panic like sirens, especially if one isn't sure what they're for. The car bombs worked the same way; she'd rig a car to explode enough just to crash and cause other accidents. If the car was parked, the windows would blow out, something people in the area found very disturbing. She couldn't know where the car would be, so she just had to hope Helena and Isabella weren't around when it happened. Those two worked mainly at night, so Kate rigged the cars to blow during the daylight hours. And LA is a big place; the three had divided it up to get maximum effect with minimum effort. There were only three of them after all. But they were running low on supplies, so it was good news that the shipment had finally arrived in Los Angeles.

The Secure Borders Project ammo drop was in a run-down industrial park near LAX. Helena waited in the car while Isabella and Kate used their charm on the defenders of the border. Isabella didn't give a damn about the border, and never gave it a thought. Kate felt the same way, but had thought about it a lot; she'd read history at Oxford and knew borders meant nothing to time and empire. She'd tried to explain this to her American colleagues at lunch, but their eyes had glazed over so she dropped it. Viola would understand her better, but there would be so much to talk about when Viola arrived.

There was no answer at the front glass doors with "Secure Plumbing and Heating" etched on them, so they strolled around the building. Isabella had a better stroll for being in sensible shoes and a nondescript Danny & Nichole suit she'd bought at Sears. Even Helena said Isabella ought to steal better clothes than that, but Isabella said she wasn't much of a hunter. This was an allusion to Kate's penchant for following well-dressed women home for their wardrobes. Better dressed, Kate kept pace with Isabella in her high heels and a houndstooth Oscar de la Renta suit as they rounded the building. Isabella took off one of her flats and pounded on the smaller metal door set in a huge door a truck could be driven into. They knew for fact that a truck had been driven in there just that morning.

A weaselly little guy opened the door. He looked surprised to see two mature women standing there. "Uh...can I help you ladies?" he asked, slack-jawed and stupid.

"Maybe," Isabella drawled, shoving past him. "Who's in charge here?" Having once been a nice lady from Atlanta, her drawl was far from intimidating. Helena had worked with her on it until they were both satisfied she could inflect her way through any situation.

The weasel stared at her like an armadillo in the headlights and then started to stutter when he fell under Kate's bland, murderous stare. "I–I...um–"

A voice boomed from the mezzanine. "What's going on, Larry?"

"Th–these ladies want to see you, Martin," Larry squeaked out.

"What do they want?"

"Well, it sure as hell ain't Avon calling," Isabella yelled. "My people were very generous with you, now it's time to hear the rest of the deal."

Martin's paunch preceded him and the glare off his pate nearly blinded the two women. But the Luger in his belt and the paranoia in his blue eyes suited them just fine. "And what can I do for you ladies?" he asked after he chased Larry off.

"We're here to discuss the best use of the weapons and explosives you got this morning, sir, and don't try to tell me you didn't," Isabella said. "You know as well as I do that a semi rolled up here at six and unloaded crates marked as heating and plumbing supplies, and was gone by nine. The Imperial Wizard appreciates your efforts on behalf of a more secure and pure America."

"And who might you be?" he asked, reeling a little from how much this woman knew about his day, but still playing it cool.

"I'm Mary Anne Evans and this is Marlene Lamarr," Isabella said.

"Our people also appreciate the efforts of the Minutemen for a more secure and pure America," Kate's voice was monotone and her posture ramrod straight. "And your efforts for the White Race have not gone unnoticed by those in authority. Our organization contributed to this morning's shipment and I am here to offer what assistance is needed."

"The Aryan Nations have sent you one of their best advisors," Isabella told Martin, who was looking a little pale. "Maybe we could sit down someplace and talk."

He ushered them into the unused front offices. "I'm not sure I like being visited by the Klan and the Nations," Martin said, scratching his pate.

"I'm sure you'll like being murdered in your bed by Negro and Latino revolutionaries when the time comes," Isabella said. "And the time's a'comin' quicker'n y'all know," she added ominously.

"Uh...m, I didn't know your organizations had women in them," he said stupidly

"You're welcome to ask your contacts about us," Isabella said. "Likely they won't know or admit who we are. That's how important our mission to Los Angeles is."

"And, uh, what is your mission?" he asked.

"To save Southern California from enemies within and without," Isabella said. "Our organizations are a little better informed than those on the ground, like yours, fighting the good fight in the trenches, and it's come to our attention that Los Angeles is going to be a flashpoint in the coming race war. This city is always on a racial knife-edge, only a little shove would send it over that edge into bloody frenzy. It's up to the Secure Border Project to be the bulwark against multicultural chaos. It's also up to your organization to give Marlene and I the support we need to root out the dangerous elements that didn't get past you on the border, but have come in from the ports. If we can find the nerve centers of their operations and destroy them, we won't need any large scale action on your part."

"Uh...what or, who–"

"These names won't mean anything to you, Martin, if I may call you Martin," Kate interjected. "The chatter we've intercepted has named several organizations working under two umbrella groups. One is the Black Crusaders and the other is La Mano Negra Frente Mexicana De Liberación, the LMNFMDL. We suspect both of these groups have infiltrated student and arts organization in this city, as well receiving aid and comfort from the FLDS, who are in a total war with the United States of America."

"What's the FLDS?" Martin asked, his jaw hanging open.

"Fundamentalist Latter Day Saints," Isabella said briskly. "Something about those one-man-one-wife laws bothers 'em a lot. Many of them live down in Mexico and have been able to use their multinational status to benefit the LMNFMDL, which has made a pact with the Black Crusaders and their drug and arms networks to loot, rape, and overall destroy the richest city on the West Coast. Shocking, I know, but I never said it was a pretty situation."

"But– but why?" Martin managed to get out. "It's

an election year, for God's sake."

"Why not, Martin?" Isabella said. "The United States government is stretched to the breaking point. If not now, there might never be a better time to overthrow at least Los Angeles, if not the whole West Coast."

"Martin," Kate said softly. She leaned forward to put her hand on his and show off her still impressive cleavage and her gun under her suit jacket. "Are you with us? We need you. We need you very much."

Although Martin admitted nothing, in the end he gave them a key to the warehouse and told his people to let Ms. Evans and Ms. Lamarr and any of their people take whatever they pleased from the latest shipment. He and Larry also carried several handpicked boxes of guns, ammo and explosives out to their Lincoln Town Car. They'd cleaned the body out of the trunk earlier that day for this very reason.

"That didn't take too long," Helena said as she drove them away.

"Let's hope he remains convinced and doesn't change the locks," Kate said, examining the keys.

"What lock has ever stopped us?" Helena asked.

"True, true, but we need his people, even if his brain is useless to us," Isabella said. "D'you think he'll look into what we said?"

"I wonder," Kate said. "He looked like he believed us."

"Well, your yarn does jive with his worst fears, doesn't it?" Helena asked. "And when he checks the internet, Miranda's already got rumors circulating that'll back you up."

"How'd we ever do anything before the internet?" Isabella asked rhetorically.

"I can't remember, seems like we talked on the phone a lot more," Helena said as she slowed to catch a red light. "Where to for the night, girls?"

"Some secluded beach house," Kate said. "I'm tired of those pretentious mansions in the hills." She looked at her nails. "And I have enough clothes for a few days."

"So, what she want to know today?" Bishop asked as he and Samsa walked Drew back to their cell.

"She wanted to know if I regretted anything," Drew said, pensively.

"And what'd ya say?" Samsa tactlessly asked. Bishop had been more respectful of Drew's feelings and planned to ask him later when they were alone.

"I said I regretted being in jail," Drew said with a sigh. "That seemed to piss her off."

They were silent for the rest of the short trek to Bishop and Drew's cell. Bishop took up his usual post at the door while Drew and Samsa sat on the lower bunk, ostensibly for Drew to jerk his bodyguard off, but lately all Samsa wanted to do was talk. Drew seemed willing enough to do just that.

"There is something I kind of regret," he said to Samsa. "I kind of regret leaving Baku. Kind of seems like a dream now."

After a giant fight with his long-suffering mother in Prague, Drew packed his laptop and went to stay in Budapest with an online gamer he'd met in Electricland. The gamer, who called himself Mussolini online, didn't have much floor for Drew to sleep on, but did hook him up with another gamer in Baku: a guy who went by Hitler in Electricland and needed somebody for his online import-export business. After a few days at Hitler's place, Drew found a tiny room in a "secure" building and began to work with contacts in Cambodia and Thailand moving shipments from point A to point B. He became very skilled at connecting people with product to people with cash; working with warehouses and hotels that didn't ask questions, and covering his tracks by sliding in and out of insecure and seemingly secure networks, many of them in the Untied States. One of the Electricland gamers who went by the name Reagan was able to help him quite a lot with some of this.

Drew was under no illusions that he was smuggling drugs and laundering money, but in his downtime he was beginning to wonder what, other than ass-kickingly addictive, Electricland really was. The game was based on an old, old book called "Neuromancer." Players went on a constantly changing variety of quests in various cyberspaces, each successful quest leading to a more complex and challenging environment. This was good because the first environment looked like a shoebox and the quest was about either stealing treasure from some kind of craft-making organization or burning their factory down. Or something; players could never go back and check what they'd done any more than they could go ahead to check what they were going to do. When Drew started playing Electricland in Prague, he thought it was kind of stupid, but its progressive strangeness and difficulty kept him coming back. Every time he logged onto the secure server and slipped into his Klaarance character, unraveling the total chaos of whatever scenario he was dumped into gave him a huge adrenaline rush. There were a lot of players, but the core group: Hitler, Mussolini, Stalin, Dutch, Overlord, Mandrake, himself, and Reagan were the main ones he interacted with. Especially Reagan: he seemed to be the most advanced player in the group, a laid-back leader of their rag-tag cyber-fellowship.

Of course Reagan's natural leadership and machismo brought out the worst in Klaarance and he began to look for Reagan's weaknesses and ways to undermine him. In moments of clarity, when he'd had enough sleep and protein, Drew realized he was becoming obsessive about the game and paranoid in general. He tried to get out more, but the crowds and traffic in Baku gave him sensory overload and quickly drove him back inside. Reagan loomed so large in Klaarance's world, Drew began to feel as if Klaarance and Reagan were more real than he himself, his seldom-seen neighbors, or anything outside the game. Reagan told him everything he wanted to hear, how strong and smart and beautiful Klaarance was. But Klaarance realized Reagan was saying that to all the gamers in Electricland. So now he had jealousy to fuel his new quest: hacking Reagan's network.

Unfortunately he succeeded. But by that time, he was so deeply in love with John Reid, he couldn't have cared less about Reagan's network. Except that John was very interested in it and Electricland.

Chapter 6

Andrew of Baku

"Excuse me, Agent Titania, but what is the point of Electricland?" the Section Manager asked.

"We're a very small unit, sir," Titania said. "We can only do so much on our own to mine the internet. So, the most efficient method was to trick clever gamers and hackers into doing it for us in what they think is a game: Electricland."

"And this works?" her Department Manager asked.

"Ninety-nine point ninety-nine percent of the time," Titania said. "This one failure was that we underestimated Ryan's intelligence and recklessness. But he was one of the best Electricland mules we had, and we don't like to throw away anything until we've wrung it bone dry." But the events of that one screw-up caused her to question whether the fruits of the internet were still worth the risk. The bottleneck in Kabul had been bad, very bad, but the unforeseen consequences of the solution had been worse. She couldn't completely blame Miranda's recklessness when she weighed it against her own concern for Hermia's operation in Laos. And it was undeniable that they all wanted to kill Williams so badly, it had become more of a need than a desire.

"Were it simple, I would have solved it by now," Hermia snarled into her phone. She blotted her brow; it was humid in Laos at that time of year. Standing on the veranda, looking over her compound with her remaining eye, she felt safe for the moment. If she could string those moments into hours or days, she'd thank a God she didn't believe in. At the moment she was too angry

for insecurity. She turned her entire body to the right to
watch a truck roll into the courtyard. It would be full of
weapons and explosives; one of the last shipments based
on a deal that was in great danger of logistical failure.
"Were it as easy as running a script, the product would
be on its way to Moscow by now. But I can't get it past
Dushanbe now."

"The hold-up is in Kabul," Titania said, her
soothing tone grating on Hermia's nerves. "We're
fixing it."

"Good." Hermia snapped her phone shut and went
down to take inventory of the weapons delivery.
Whoever was stealing from the Americans and selling to
her had exquisite taste in war materiel.

The U.S. insignia always made her feel cold. It
reminded Hermia of the time she spent being
interrogated and mutilated by "contractors." Such an
easy word, such an easy way for the Americans to deny
what true monsters they'd become since September 11.
If not before, if not always. At least they didn't use
water on her. After the tsunami that took everything
from her, she'd never completely overcome her horror
of being immersed in water. The knives and hot irons
didn't break her, even when she could hear her own eye
being destroyed, but if they'd waterboarded her, she
would have died or gone mad very quickly.

Hermia picked up an Anaconda revolver and a
speed loader. The heft and balance appealed to her.
She hated the Americans, but she liked their guns; she
especially liked killing them with their own guns. But
after indulging in one test round, Hermia put the gun
away and turned her mind back to the bottleneck in
Dushanbe, or rather, in Kabul as Titania seemed to
think. She was inclined to believe Titania was right and
would solve it. Titania had so many resources at her
disposal in and out of Electricland.

"Kate's on her way to Kabul to kill him," Titania said
tensely into her phone. "Go there and back her up. And

one of you get the opium moving for Hermia. Our e-mules can't get the real mules past Blackwater for some reason."

"Do you think he's onto Hermia?" Viola's voice was very small over the internet scramble.

"Maybe, but one small drug and arms operation is nothing to him," Titania said flatly.

"Except that it's Hermia's operation." Viola needlessly reminded her. "She's all the guilt he has, and he won't rest until she's dead."

"He's as incapable of guilt as he is of love, Viola," Titania said wearily. "If I thought he was going to track Hermia to Laos, I'd fly over and watch her kill him slowly."

"We all would," Viola assured her. "She's our guilt, too, Titania. We didn't get her out quickly enough. I know that—"

"Viola, penetrating a secure position takes time," Titania cut her off. "We were lucky the Americans and their 'contractors' didn't know what or whom we were really after."

"Yes, of course, but—"

"We don't have time for regrets today, Viola, just go kill him and then get to Baku and take out that little bastard Ryan. Miranda will have a C4 supplier for you when you get there. I'm hanging up now." Titania broke the connection and looked sternly at Miranda. "Yes? And?" she briskly asked the top of the obese hacker's head.

"Klaarance has some miles left on him," Miranda said, not looking away from her screens. "It's wasteful to throw him away now."

"He's out of control, Miranda," Titania said softly. "You've lost control of him. He's challenging you, and you're too overextended to slap him back into submission. He has to be removed from Electricland. You said so yourself. And you have got to get those drugs moving east, west, and north from Tajikistan."

"Klaarance is working on it," Miranda said smugly.

"Are you out of your mind?" Titania didn't bother to modulate the horror in her voice.

"The operation he works for is using all the mules from Kabul to Bishkek," Miranda said. "I've hacked into Klaarance's– sorry, Ryan's network to move a few of his mules to work for us. I will be in and out before he realizes he's been hacked."

"Are you insane?" Titania asked, but her voice was softer; insanity might be useful in this situation.

"He won't even know I was in there," Miranda said dreamily. "He's just a kid. He's not that smart."

"Since you've already done it, I hope you're right," Titania said, resigned and already thinking of the next thing on her endless to-do list.

"I am right. And after you kill him, I'll stay in his network and put them out of business, too," Miranda said as if it were already a fait accompli.

"Good, fine. Just do whatever you have to do in Central Asia so you can focus on Irvine next." Titania patted a non-existent stray hair back into her perfect blond coif. "But for God's sake, Miranda, if that little swine Ryan messes up my schedule anymore, I'll go out there and kill him myself."

Viola wore her years and sorrow with grace and urbanity. Sitting in a Baku café watching Ryan's building, waiting for him to show up, waiting for Miranda to find her a safe C4 supplier—she wouldn't need very much to blow up one little computer freak, but she did need some—she was a very charming picture and had already very charmingly rebuffed a few advances: one in French, two in Russian. A rebuff from Viola was more like a caress from anyone else. Most people who met her, however briefly, were calmed and enchanted by her tranquil charm and aura of peace and wisdom befitting a woman of her age. She'd adopted this pose to cover her agony and hatred for a world she'd done everything to placate, but that had still taken everything from her. Except her life, the one thing that meant nothing to her, and then, as the supreme joke, God, fate, luck, or whatnot would not allow her to throw it away.

After working as an analyst for a covert operation of the Direction Générale de la Sécurité Extérieure, Viola went home to Beirut, fell in love and settled down to raise a family. But after her family and friends where murdered by Israeli bombs and not one voice was raised against it in the civilized world or the United States, Viola became a killer for Hamas. They'd originally offered her a suicide bomber deal, but she quickly convinced them she could kill more people in other, less chaotic, fashions. At that moment, Viola, before she became Viola, released her wrath against the world that had broken her heart and cast her aside.

While waiting for the mysterious Andrew Ryan/Klaarance creature to materialize, Viola had the leisure to sip her tea and muse on Titania's obsession with Warren Williams. Of course they all wanted to kill him for abandoning Hermia to those monsters, but Viola suspected that Titania's grudge went back farther than that. Viola had met Titania in Chechnya before Titania became Titania. Hamas had sent Viola to train the Black Widows, women like herself who had nothing to lose, but were more suicidal in their world view. Viola could admire the sacrifice of a suicide bomber, but not the waste, and being practical even in her rage, she was more homicidal than suicidal.

The Black Widows were more like herself than the Syrians she'd been working with, and mission training them had almost been a pleasure. Viola didn't kid herself: however well she trained them, these women didn't stand a chance against the Russian security machine. No one was even sure the Chechens were behind the bombing in Moscow that conveniently led to the invasion and rape of Chechnya, which led to women losing everything, which led to the Black Widows, who would die for revenge, which isn't the worst thing in the world to die for. The worst thing in the world to die for is an unworthy cause, and Viola considered the Black Widows above all that. They were going to die for a very worthy cause. They were terrorist tsarinas, Kamikazes, a cavalry charge into machine guns, and Viola wished them well for what was left of their short lives.

And Viola would have liked to have forgotten about them, too, but she was detained by American advisors outside of Tbilisi and interviewed—because it was nothing like an interrogation—by a woman who'd come to study the Black Widows.

Her inner calm intact, Viola assured the composed woman on the other side of the desk that she was merely a harmless aid worker based in Yerevan on her way back there after a humanitarian mission to the people of Chechnya. The woman behind the desk then assured her that it certainly looked that way, but her group had been tracking her since she arrived in Chechnya, so they knew she'd been working with the Black Widows.

"I came here to study the Black Widows," Titania said pleasantly. "America is trying to understand the terrorist mind to combat it more effectively." This was a lie, but the smile that went with it was so charming, it wouldn't have mattered if it was the truth.

"How admirable," Viola lied with equal sweetness. Her experience with Americans combating terrorists was less analytical and, fortunately, less efficient. When the war president blew up a city full of women and children it was war; when Viola blew up a truck full of soldiers, it was terrorism. Of course neither of them got their hands dirty, but Viola's motives did not involve making anyone's penis larger. Rather the reverse. "But I assure you, madam, I was merely in Chechnya delivering medical supplies."

"Yes, crates marked as medical supplies, but full of this sort of thing." Titania held up an APB revolver with a shoulder stock and a Korshon knife. "One of your widows got careless after you left them. Not terribly careless; she killed two of my associates on her way to glory. I would say you're an excellent teacher." Titania ordered the guard out of the room when Viola glanced at him.

"I would say there was a note of envy in those words, sister," Viola said softly. "You came here to die, didn't you?"

"My reasons for being here are not–"

"I wonder," Viola cooed. "Why do the men in charge send an old woman to study violence? Shouldn't you be home tending grandchildren and baking apple pies?"

"You know noth–"

"Then tell me: why are you here?" Viola leaned back to listen.

"This is my field," Titania said bitterly. "I'm a terrorism analyst. No one listens to me, but I do have to turn in reports on something to keep my salary and health insurance." Her hand came down firmly on the knife when Viola's eyes strayed to it. "When I heard the first rumors of the Black Widows, I proposed a team to study them. My country is responsible for quite a bit of collateral damage, there's bound to be blowback, and some of it might be female."

"Yes, kill a woman's family and friends, destroy her home. Difficult to know what she'll do," Viola said coldly. "You Americans ought to take a lesson from the Russians: in Afghanistan they were losers, in Chechnya they're winners, in both places they were and are monsters. Their victims, like your victims, have no army, but they have one life and many lives they can take with that one life."

"Your English is perfect," Titania observed. "Where did you learn it?"

"In Lebanon and then at university in France," Viola said. "Where did you learn yours?"

"America."

"How many languages do you speak?"

"Four. You?"

"Eight and some dialects, but I wasn't raised in a

monoculture," Viola said.

"With your looks and education, may I ask why you're doing this?" Titania asked, folding her hands on the desk.

"I could ask you the same question," Viola said. "You've the air of a woman who could do anything."

"And someday I might, but for now, this is my job. And you?"

Viola examined the woman before her and found it disturbingly like looking in a mirror. She shrugged. "I died with my family and friends some years ago," she said slowly. "My body is just trying to catch up with my soul." She looked away from the raw emotion ghosting across her interlocutor's face. Viola was unarmed, but she wasn't worried. This woman was her equal, her peer, her sister-in-arms; if the woman behind the desk with the knife and the gun killed her, she'd be doing her a very large favor. When the silence had gone on for too long, she looked back and found Titania's eyes had gone dead again. "I think you are the same."

"I think...if you go now, I can cover up that you were ever here," Titania said slowly after a few moment of staring into the other woman's eyes. And then she looked down.

Viola was on her with the knife at her throat in one motion. "Be careful," she whispered into Titania's frozen face. "It's compassion that also kills. Here's something to remind you of the lesson." The blade was razor sharp and drew a thin, shallow line on Titania's left cheek in the dermis from her zygomatic bone to her jawbone. "Adieu." Viola picked up the submachine gun and left.

When they met again, Titania had no scar on her cheek. She said she'd had it removed when she had her facelift. Her offer of a job killing Americans and their allies, funded by the U.S. government, was irresistible to Viola. And also to Kate, who'd joined Viola's terrorist cell a few weeks before. They were both too well-educated and well-bred to continue to take orders from fanatical men intent on making them wear bags over the chic clothes and trim figures they worked so hard to maintain, so Titania's offer was fortuitous. And her forged documents for the two women were flawless. The Shakespearian code names were a little silly, but Viola and Kate, unlike Desdemona and Ophelia, at least survived their plays.

"You're not the same," Viola observed on the boat to Cypress.

"No, not the same," Titania sighed. "I'm a woman with a woman-owned small business with extramural funding to combat terrorism now. Completely different from a government employee."

"'Combat terrorism'?" Kate asked.

"My grant proposal didn't specify what kind of terrorism. And, as we know, there are all kinds of terrorism. Some of which has to be fought with terrorism."

"Fighting fire with fire," Kate said nodding.

"Yes, at least that's my story and I'm sticking to it," Titania said, and ushered them downstairs for tea and into a new life.

Back in Baku, Viola wondered how many years she'd spent drinking tea and waiting for someone or something. Well, at least Ryan was cute in a certain scruffy way when he did show up. She gave him time to get to his hovel and followed him into the building.

It was a wreck inside, as she'd expected. Even with her frail, womanly physique she could have punched through the door. However, she would have had difficulty punching through the huge hall guard. "Just here to see a friend," she told the brute in English, then French, then Western Armenian, then finally Russian, which he decided he could understand. The crisp twenty-dollar bill might have had something do with the improvement in his comprehension as well. By that time, Drew and a few other denizens had opened their doors to see what was going on in the hall. "I have a message for you, Klaarance," she said, suppressing a mental giggle at the ridiculous name he'd chosen for himself. "From Reagan."

Looking over the scrawny kid standing before her, Viola could not but wonder at the amount of trouble the little monster had caused them. According to Miranda, he'd become a problem in the Electricland game, a problem the real world would have to get rid of for her. Klaarance was a dangerous fool in Electricland. But the words "Jesters do oft prove prophets," ran through Viola's mind. Too bad that was said by a Regan, not a Reagan. Foolish Lear, giving away his power and expecting compassion and respect in his powerless state. Viola thought it should be listed under the comedies; she thought it had a very happy ending.

"Who are you? What do you want?" Ryan squeaked at her, dragging her out of her literary musing.

"I want," she said fixing him with her sexiest stare, "to come in." She brushed past him and closed the door. There wasn't much room in the tiny windowless space, just enough for a cot and a desk with several computers on it. She noticed a filthy sink, but nothing resembling a bath. "My God," she thought. "I should kill him now before he has to spend another second in this rat hole." But Miranda and Titania were adamant that she must blow him up—if enough C4 could be found in Baku—to obliterate all traces of him. Miranda was too fond of words like obliterate, annihilate, eviscerate; Viola assumed it was the overblown vocabulary of Electricland and felt free to sneer at it.

However, at that moment she almost felt sorry for the young man slouching before her. "Reagan sent you some money," she said, tossing an envelope on the desk and taking a seat on the cot where she could survey the room for good places to plant the explosives.

Ryan opened the envelope and thumbed through the bills. "Why?" he asked.

"I've no idea, I'm just the messenger girl," Viola leaned back at an angle flattering to her figure. She began to feel annoyed when Ryan merely looked puzzled, and not intrigued. "What are you going to do with that money?" she asked, and got a shrug for her trouble. "Why not show me around Baku?" she suggested. "I've never been here before." Technically this was true: she'd only passed through Baku, she'd never been stuck there before.

"There's nothing to see here," Ryan muttered.

"Really?" Viola asked.

"I...I don't go out much," he muttered some more.

"Oh, well, then let me show you my hotel at least." She made it sound like a suggestion.

"Um..."

"I'm here alone for a few days, Klaarance," she said smoothly. "You're the only one I know here."

"Uh..."

"Are you hungry?" she asked.

"Am I hungry?" he asked back.

"Yes, hungry," she said, smiling. "I'm starving. There's a good restaurant in my hotel. At least come have something to eat with me. I hate to eat alone. Don't you hate to eat alone?" she asked, eyeing the stale bread and cheese by the computers.

"I– uh, yeah, I guess," he said after staring at her for a while. "Okay. But only if you promise to tell me about Reagan."

"I'll tell you everything I know," Viola said, enjoying the frisson of pleasure at the prospect of the outrageous lies she would tell him.

"What's your name?" he asked, shoving a laptop into a shoulder bag.

"Oh, just call me Mademoiselle," she said, leading him out of his hovel. She even bestowed a gracious nod on the thug in the hallway on their way out.

On the way to her hotel, Viola got a whiff of him in the taxi and began to think up tactful ways to get him to take a shower. She also got a call from Titania telling her where the C4 would be delivered. She got such a strange look from the driver when she told him their new destination, she missed what Titania was saying.

Ginger Mayerson

"Répéte, s'il te plaît?"

"I said, this is someone we know from Georgia," Titania repeated in French.

"Really? I've never been in that hellhole— Oh wait, which Georgia?" Viola smiled pleasantly at Ryan who appeared not to be understanding their conversation. French got more decorative and less useful every year, alas.

"The Georgia I met you in," Titania said. "One of your trainees decided to forego a noble death in favor of an immoral life."

"How unusual," Viola said, distracted by the deteriorating neighborhood they were entering. No wonder the driver looked weird when she gave him the address. "Who is it?"

"I met her there after I met you there. She was a fund of useless information, hysterics, and rage, but gave me quite a bit of insight into what not to do with my future project," Titania said. "She's going by Valentina Alexandrova now, but she used to call herself Looli."

Viola was trying to remember who Looli was; she made it a policy to never get too attached to any of her trainees. She was also wondering how safe seeing someone from her past was. The taxi stopped in front of a large decrepit house; Viola double-checked the address with Titania before she hung up on her. She took a deep breath and began to convince the driver to wait for her when the large front door opened and a middle-aged woman with long dark hair wearing a tight black dress over her wide hips with a fuchsia bolero jacket above them came down the steps to the taxi. She kept her hands in plain sight, one of which had a wad of bills that she gave to the driver. "Looli," Viola thought, remembering the lovely widow who was still too numb from losing her family to channel her rage. Viola had figured Looli wouldn't last long as a Black Widow. Apparently she hadn't lasted long at all if she was in Baku running around under the name of Valentina

Alexandrova. "How kind of you to pay the driver, Madame," Viola said, switching to Russian.

"It is my pleasure, Mademoiselle," Valentina said warmly. "It's always a pleasure to help a sister-in-arms. And who is this young man?"

Viola introduced Ryan, who only spoke the most rudimentary Russian, which suited Viola fine. Once inside the rambling wreck of a house, which was lushly furnished and decorated, Viola was even more pleased to learn it was a whorehouse. "Never judge a house by its door," she thought as Valentina led them to a tea table. "Do you think a few of your girls could give my boy a bath?" she asked.

Valentina rang for her maid, who smiled so wickedly Viola had to make it clear whose boy he was. The girl dropped her a charming curtsey and left the room. She came back with three other girls, not unlike herself: young, well-fed and saucy.

"Klaarance, my dear, you need a bath," Viola said in English. "And these girls are going to give it to you."

"What!" was all Ryan got out before he was swept away by the pack of giggling girls.

Viola yelled after them to bring down his clothes so they could be washed. "I suppose you can bill Titania for whatever this bath and the room is going to cost," Viola said to Valentina when the giggling and struggling were out of earshot.

"It's on the house, Mademoiselle," Valentina said. "I would, however, prefer that you remove the package that was delivered today as soon as you can." She set a plaid plastic tote bag by Viola's feet.

"Of course, if you'll lend me a car and keep my boy here," Viola said, sipping tea and taking inventory of the bag, while Valentina went to see about the car: C4, detonator, wireless receiver, remote detonator, and a Kahr PM9 pistol and Scorpion silencer. She transferred the explosives to her shoulder bag and put the pistol in her pocket with an extra magazine. "Ah," she said as a large man came in with Ryan's clothes. "I hope he's not being too much trouble," she said, and just got a grunt, so she wasn't sure if he'd understood her or not. She riffled through Ryan's nasty clothes until she found his keys.

Valentina came back and said the car was ready; she poked at the pile of nearly rags that were Ryan's clothes. "Shall we wash them?" she asked.

"Rather you'd burn them," Viola said, hoisting her shoulder bag. "But first replace them with something nicer." She tossed some money on the table. "Let me know if that's not enough and get the little fool some new shoes as well." She added more money to the pile. "Tell him that's what I'm doing, buying him new clothes, just don't let him leave before I get back," she said, following Valentina down to a Fiat sedan. The large man who'd come in with Ryan's clothes earlier was at the wheel.

The driver knew his city and how to drive it so he got Viola to Ryan's hovel very quickly. She slipped up the stairs and jingled Ryan's keys at the hallway guard, who scowled at her over a vile-looking sandwich, but did nothing else. Inside Ryan's room, Viola wedged the explosives between his computer desk and the wall. It was a lot of C4, so it would do the job from there; hell, it would probably do the job if she planted it on the floor below. She kept the remote detonator and let herself out, waved cheerfully to the hallway creature and glided down the stairs.

She got back to Valentina's place in time to help her former protégé pick out a tasteful ensemble from the clothing vendor who made brothel calls. Between the three of them, they put together a very nice outfit, including an overcoat, of subdued blacks and grays that wouldn't show dirt and would set off Ryan's pallor very nicely. The best they could do on shoes were some sneakers. Viola didn't feel too bad about this since he wouldn't be wearing any of it right away and then not for very long afterwards.

On her way up to the room where the freshly

scrubbed Ryan was fuming, as Valentina informed her, Viola figured she'd let Titania know when Ryan left her. She headed upstairs with just one thing on her mind. But when she got there, she just had a hard time not laughing at the angry young man in a floral robe that was too small for him. He stopped swearing at her when she tossed him the bundle of clothes.

There was a plate of open-face sandwiches, some cucumber and bell pepper salad, and a bowl of fruit on a table. Viola merely noticed them as she picked up the bottle of Tamada Saperavi wine next to them. Out of their meager funds, the Black Widows had treated her to a bottle or two. They claimed Chechen wine was far superior, but the war had destroyed so many vineyards... "The war," she thought, "has destroyed more than that." Memory rushed up on her, so much suffering for those widows, but they would not simply die: they had fought and then died. And, now, in a Baku whorehouse, Viola could only stare at the bottle in her hands and feel rage that looked like sorrow, tears of fury that would not fall, but glittered on her lashes. She was aware that Klaarance had stopped swearing and was standing half-dressed before her.

"Um, are you okay?" he asked, stooping a little more, trying to see her face.

"Oh, I'm okay, I am," she said, brushing away a tear. "I was just remembering how good this wine was. Is there a corkscrew?" Klaarance found one on the table and then, at her request, awkwardly opened the wine. "Have something to eat. I promised you food, it's the least I can do."

"I'm not a prisoner, am I?" he asked, eyeing her, the food and the door in a shifty rotation.

"No." She laughed. "I'm sorry about the bath. I just couldn't resist."

"Well...it was kind of fun..." He sat down and started stuffing his face.

Viola sat next to him, waiting for the wine to breathe. "I'm sorry I missed it." He asked her to tell him about Reagan. "Ah, you haven't forgotten," she said cheerfully, thinking up what lies she'd add to what she did know about Miranda. One of the reasons Titania kept Miranda close to her is that the hacker liked to talk too much. The one time Miranda met Viola, she'd spilled her rather large guts. But people had a habit of pouring their hearts out to Viola and she was skilled at leading them along until they told her everything she wanted to know. She considered Ryan too young to be interesting, except for sex. "I don't know very much about Reagan. There are rumors that he's quite brilliant and gigantically fat."

"I heard he's a math genius," Ryan said, chomping away at a sandwich. "But I didn't know he was fat."

"Oh, huge, very huge," she said, smiling. "Or so I'm told, but I'm just a lowly messenger for him."

"You seem kind of...um..."

"Old for the job?" she asked with a laugh in her voice.

"Sophisticated, yeah, sophisticated for the job," he said, smiling at her for the first time. "I mean, the way you dress and talk."

"Why, thank you, Klaarance," she said, almost touched by his sweet smile and coltish forthrightness, even though she thought he was an idiot for admiring her dark brown, easy-care, wrinkle-resistant, cheap rayon travel skirt and jacket. He asked her to tell him more about Reagan/Miranda, and she spun him a tale that was mostly true. "Reagan was always a misfit," she said. "Too smart, rather ugly, and physically weak. You know how the strong prey on the weak unless they can be used for pleasure or labor or both. Of course there are laws that are supposed to protect us from each other, but it's all really just game so we'll all keep playing, working, pouring money and blood in the pockets of the men in charge." She stopped because he was gaping at her. She reached across the table to stroke his chin and close his mouth. "But about Reagan, in particular, he was weak and ugly and hid in his room.

His parents were overworked barely middle-class people who drank, so he hid from them as well. Some friend or relative took pity on the poor boy and introduced him the internet computers at the local library. A new world opened before him. One evening a man in the library picked him up and offered Reagan money to masturbate in front of him. That–"

"Wait! Who's doing what?" Ryan asked tensely.

"Reagan masturbated in front of the man and got paid for it," she clarified. "That led to other similar scenes," she continued at his nod. "One day a man offered him a computer and internet connection in exchange for an exclusive...what's it called? Webcamera? Yes, webcamera arrangement. It was getting too dangerous to meet in person. Thereafter, Reagan never left his home until his parents caught him masturbating in front of his computer and threw him out. He lived with one 'protector' after another until he was caught with a high-ranking government official. He then fell into the hands of a kindly woman with a woman-owned small business who appreciated his computer skills more than his limited and specialized sexual prowess. He lives in safety now, and is almost a productive member of society."

"Oh...I thought he was more exciting," Ryan said glumly.

"Did you think he was some kind of guerrilla hacker anarchist?" she asked.

"Yes."

"Have you ever met one?" she asked.

"No."

"That's because they don't last very long," she said, getting bored. "The lone man taking on the system is a myth. A computer is no match for a gun. Society–"

"You can do a lot of damage with a computer," Ryan said smiling evilly. Or as evilly as one can smile with crumbs around one's mouth.

"You can do a lot of damage without one, too," Viola said, her interest sparked again by Ryan's cheekiness.

The room was long with shadows by then, what was left of the light was warm, golden and very flattering to Ryan. Viola slowly extended her hand to brush the crumbs off his lips. From there, she stroked his cheek and neck. He leaned into her touch so she ran her hand down his chest to his lap: he was getting hard.

Her true, loving, womanly desire had been burned out of her, but she had managed to regain something of an appetite. And just then the ridiculous boy in front of her was making her mouth water. She stroked him teasingly through his pants. "Take these off and get in bed," she sighed, and he moved like she'd barked an order.

Lighting the candle on the table and drawing the curtains, Viola felt herself soften a little. She preferred to make her conquests in the dark, thereby avoiding any questions about knife, gunshot, shrapnel, and assorted other injury scars, not to mention the C-section scars from her last two children. Although her belly sloped from her pregnancies and she had cellulite and stretch marks, her body was still warm and firm and smooth to the touch. Sliding out of her clothes and into Ryan's arms, she admired his strong embrace for someone with stick-like arms. Of course, based on the lingering clinch and sloppy, misplaced kiss, it only took Viola a few seconds to realize Ryan had no idea what to do with a woman.

Amused, she caressed her way down his torso to his respectable erection. Based on the length and heft, Viola imagined it was in proportion to his body, which, if he'd taken care of himself, might not have been a bad body at all. As it was, he was too thin and had the muscle tone of youth and that was about it.

However, Ryan's future was not much on her mind as she shoved him on his back and slid her clit and vulva along the length until she was aroused enough to ease him inside. He quit his clumsy kneading of her breasts when she began to move; he seemed to be in shock. After a minute, he snapped out of it and began to move with her. After another minute he came.

"Virgins," Viola thought with a heavy mental sigh. She lay beside him and finished herself off with her fingers. She brushed his hand away when, either out of minimal manners or curiosity, he tried to help.

"I, um, guess that should have been longer..." Ryan mumbled.

"Let's see how you do in about fifteen minutes," Viola said menacingly.

He lasted longer the second time, and longer that on the third time, which included a sixty-nine. Viola thought he had potential at cunnilingus; rather a shame he wouldn't live long enough to develop it.

After a short doze, she made sure he was sound asleep before getting into her clothes and taking his laptop bag, which still contained the envelope of money from Reagan. Ryan certainly wouldn't be needing the computer or the cash much longer. She slipped out of the room and paused to listen in the hallway. The house was in full swing with noisy clients, drinking up some courage and sex drive before taking their whore upstairs. Viola cursed and went back into the bedroom, softly closing the door. She was needlessly quiet; Ryan was out like a light, so he could hardly hear her go out the window and climb down the bars over the ground-floor window. It occurred to her that many of Looli's clients might leave her second floor bedrooms this way, and that Looli must get payment up front or she'd be out of business very soon.

Viola stayed in the shadows until she was several blocks from Looli's brothel. Then she caught a taxi to the center of the city, had a cup of tea, and caught a bus to her hotel. After having a magnum of champagne sent up to her room, she woke up Titania and Miranda via a landline relay through the Berlin Zoo and said, "All is ready."

While sipping her champagne, Viola paid careful attention to Miranda's directions for uploading the contents of Ryan's laptop to a secure server and then followed the instructions for reformatting the hard drive. As an added precaution, Viola took a walk to a secluded spot where she could toss the laptop into the Caspian.

Chapter 7

Love is the Greatest Weapon of All

"Let me understand this, Agent Titania," the Section Manager ran his hands through what was left of his hair. "Your agent, on a dangerous mission, wasted valuable time seducing her target."

"Of course," she said.

"It's disgusting," her Department Manager spat. He didn't run his hand through his hair, he clenched his fists in his lap instead. He had so little hair, running his hands through it might have been detrimental to what was still there.

"You wouldn't say that about James Bond," she said, quite reasonably. He just sneered at her.

"Well, nevertheless, I must ask why did she do it?" her Section Manager asked, equally reasonably.

"Quel est le sens d'amour?" she asked, although she knew perfectly well Viola's tryst with Ryan was motivated purely by lust. She got totally blank stares. French really was more decorative than useful nowadays.

"So, what else happened to ya in Baku?" Samsa asked, brushing Drew's hand away from his fly. They were sitting on Bishop's bunk, ostensibly so Drew could jack Samsa off, but Samsa was more interested in Drew's past in Baku. Bishop was watching the tier, trying not to look interested in what was being said a few feet away.

"I met John Reid," Drew said, sitting back. "He was the first guy I had sex with."

"I hope he was younger than the grandma who popped your cherry," Bishop growled.

"He might have been the same age," Drew said, dreamily. "Or maybe a little older. But he was really...really..."

"What's with you and these old people?" Bishop snapped.

Drew demurely lowered his eyes and didn't answer.

"He was really, really what?" Samsa asked, gently.

"Really sexy."

A lot of people owed Williams favors, or could be convinced they did. He was tall and handsome, his distinguished face framed by jet black hair graying at the temples. He was the kind of man who inspired trust and respect until he inspired fear and disgust. When he got to Baku a day after the agent he called Mademoiselle, he called in a few favors and, without naming her or explaining too much, put the word out on the woman he was looking for. His story was that she owed him a lot of money or a lot of oral sex. This story seemed satisfy the arms dealers he told it to. He knew she'd need arms because she'd flown commercial from Tashkent to Baku and left her guns behind. He'd almost lost her on the way into Uzbekistan, but one of his contacts in Dushanbe had heard of a woman traveling alone under a Russian passport heading for Moscow, via Tashkent. Clever Mademoiselle, but not clever enough: in her hurry, she'd left tracks not to Moscow, but to Baku, where she vanished.

But it was only a matter of time before she surfaced again. Titania's operatives were never unarmed for long, and lo and behold, one of Williams' reliable contacts for weapons and explosives informed him that the woman he was looking has been at a certain address at a certain time picking up a gun and C4. "What are you up to, Mademoiselle?" Williams wondered.

The reliable contact provided Williams with a car and driver and a bottle of peppermint schnapps. Sitting in the back seat of an elderly Lada sedan, Williams listened to, but couldn't understand, the driver's cell phone conversation. Williams knew quite a few languages, but wasn't familiar with language or dialect the driver was speaking. The driver turned halfway around in his seat and told Williams in Russian that the woman he was looking for had arrived a few minutes earlier. "She was not alone," the driver added, clicking his cell phone shut.

"Who was with her?" Williams asked.

"A young man. Our delivery man didn't get a good look at him," the driver said, threading his way through traffic.

"How do we know it's her?" Williams asked, making conversation.

"The madam of the whorehouse only said someone would be picking the delivery up," the driver said. "It was a woman who came here, a very beautiful older woman, our delivery man mentioned it twice."

"Huh," Williams said, but was thinking, "Yes sir, that'd be Mademoiselle." He watched the neighborhood get bleaker and bleaker around him. Seemed like an odd place for a brothel, but in his experience, each brothel location was unique unto itself, so he suspended judgment. "Oh, fuck, she's leaving already. Follow her!"

The driver was good, but Williams could tell Mademoiselle wasn't worried about being tailed. Keeping a discreet distance, the driver followed her to a crumbling apartment building where she went inside for ten minutes, and came back out. She got in the same cab and headed back to the brothel.

After making a note of the address, Williams used the driver's cell phone to call his reliable contact. "Who lives at this place?" he asked, rattling off Drew's apartment building address. The reliable contact didn't know off the top of his head, but said he'd call back. Williams and the driver were drinking peppermint schnapps and watching the whorehouse get lively with clientele when the reliable contact called back. He told Williams that the address in question was a very secure place: it had its own power generator, several satellite dishes on the roof, and guards on each floor. No one knew much about what went on inside, but the tenants had a lot of computers and other electronic equipment. They were also very quiet and seldom left the building. The operations and inhabitants of that address were poorly understood by the authorities and most of the local underworld. The building management negotiated modest bribes to useful persons. And so, as a consequence of being a low-key, well guarded place, with no obvious illegal or even lucrative activity that paid its bribes on time, it was ignored and avoided.

Williams thanked him for the information and sat back in the car wondering what the fuck Mademoiselle was doing in Baku. She was known as a killer and a terrorist. The people in the brothel and the apartment building were not the kind of targets she usually went after. He dismissed the idea she was on vacation. People like themselves never took vacations. And if she wasn't on an assignment, she would likely be somewhere in the Levant, which was where he thought she was originally from. Most of what he knew about her was rumor, speculation and deduction, but he did know she'd been in Chechnya. And that made the Chechen madam in the brothel he was watching extremely interesting.

It was boring in the car. Williams dismissed the driver and went quietly around to the kitchen door. There were a lot of places Mademoiselle might be in that house, but he figured the kitchen wasn't one of them. He asked the thug at the back door for Valentina Alexandrova and mentioned the reliable contact's name. A few minutes later Valentina Alexandrova stepped into the kitchen.

"Well, well," Williams said in Russian. "It has been a long time, Looli, hasn't it?"

"Not long enough, Mr. Williams," she said, lifting her chin and sneering at him. "What do you want?"

Due to his potent masculinity, Williams was used to

women sneering at him, so he was unmoved by this. If he wasn't working, he might have enjoyed turning her sneer into a smile, just for him. But he was working, so he adjusted his stance in case she decided to do more than sneer and attacked him with a kitchen utensil. It was a kitchen, after all. "You turned on Mademoiselle. That's why I'm here."

"If I'd known it was you, I would have kept my mouth shut," Looli said through clenched teeth.

"Yes, well, in the interconnected underworld of Baku, you did the right thing," Williams said, somewhat sick of her dramatics, although watching her impressive rack heave with every angst-ridden sigh was as delightful as ever. "Mademoiselle and I are just passing through your new home. Tell me what she's doing in Baku and where she is and I'll be on my way myself." He leaned casually against the back door.

Looli shrugged, crossed the kitchen and poured two cups of coffee. "You still drink your coffee black?" she asked, but made it sound like an accusation. She sat down at the oilcloth covered table in the middle of the room.

"As my heart, yes," he answered. "Now, talk Looli, I haven't got all night." He joined her at the kitchen table and sipped at a very good cup of coffee.

"I had a call from La Directrice this morning, asking me to give a package to Mademoiselle this afternoon," Looli said, cradling her coffee mug. "Soon after her call, a messenger delivered the package, then I got a phone call from a very powerful man in Baku asking who wanted the package. Everyone owes him a favor, including me, but I only told him I did not know who it was, but I told him when that person would be here. And now you are here."

"Very loyal, in a half-assed sort of way," Williams thought. "And Mademoiselle?" he prompted.

"She arrived with a boy," Looli said slowly. "I thought she was here to just pick up the package and go, but she told us to keep the boy here until she came back.

They have been in Room 8 since she got back this afternoon."

"A...a boy?" Williams was nonplussed.

This was as much of a break as Looli needed. She threw her hot coffee in his face and grabbed a knife off the counter. She missed his throat but put a good gash in his shoulder. Unable to dodge, she was stunned by his left hook to her chin. She hardly noticed him breaking her neck.

"Fuck!" Williams dragged Looli's rather ample form into the pantry and hoped no one would find her until he was gone. He wiped the coffee off his face and used the dishtowel for a compress on his shoulder. It gave him a hunchback appearance, but he was vain enough to think it made him edgily attractive.

Trying to look casual, Williams strolled into the subdued whorehouse parlor. It was quiet because it was late enough for everyone to be upstairs fucking. One of the maids was wiping down a couch and gave him a curious look, but didn't try to stop him from going upstairs. There was a thug lounging on the landing who did that.

"Madam told me to get the kid out of number 8," Williams said, as he shelled out three crisp twenties.

The thug just grunted and pocketed the cash. He did helpfully indicate with his chin that room number 8 was to the left of the landing.

Williams might have figured this out on his own because there were numbers on the doors. He drew his gun and slipped into the unlocked room.

The first thing that hit him was Mademoiselle's perfume: a blend of jasmine, rose and musk that cascaded right down a man's spine, tickled his balls, and glided back up again. It was a subtle trio of civilized scents, yet very powerful in combination. Had Williams been a less disciplined man, he might have lingered a little longer in the memories that seductive fragrance trigged, but he was working. The reason he lingered at all was that that particular perfume was usually mixed with the smell of death, or at least blood, and neither of those were present in the dark bedroom.

There was a lump in the bed; presumably living, unless she'd found a tidier way to kill people, but it was hard to tell in the flickering light from the candles gutting out. Williams cat-footed it across the room and took a seat on the edge of the bed. Unable to see properly, he turned on the bedside lamp. Shaded in a deep rose, the low-watt bulb gave off enough light to see the gaunt profile of the young man in the bed. It was enough light to wake the kid, too, and he bolted up with a start.

"Who the fuck are you?" he snarled, clutching the covers to his chest. "And where the hell—"

"She's gone," Williams cut him off. "I'm Reid, John Reid. Who are you?"

"Andrew Ryan," Drew said, looking around. In another second he was out of the bed, rummaging around the room naked. "Fuck! Where's my laptop?"

"Like I said, she's gone," Williams said, and hearing a commotion downstairs, grabbed a chair and jammed it under the doorknob. "And we should be going, too."

There were heavy boots, shouting, screaming, and gunshots inside and outside the house. Drew was too confused to find his clothes, so Williams wrapped the chenille bedspread around him and shoved him into the wardrobe. Not a moment too soon; the brothel thugs didn't bother knocking. They shot the door to pieces.

Betting on his luck, like always, Williams kept one hand on Drew and the other on his gun. Luckily, the thugs rushed into the room, saw the open window, assumed they'd climbed down, and went racing downstairs.

Although Williams was enjoying the way the kid smelled at close range—a combination of Mademoiselle's perfume, sex, and his own youthful musk—he judged they might not be able to get out without a little help. He called his reliable contact and asked for an escort back to his hotel. A big escort.

While waiting for the rescue, Williams pocketed his gun, and pulled Drew close, telling him not to worry.

"I'm not worried," Drew said, edging away in the tight space.

"But you're trembling," Williams said, finding this coyness irresistible. "Don't be afraid." He'd never been this close to one of Mademoiselle's lovers—mostly he found them dead—and he was smitten and intrigued in equal measures.

"I'm not scared," Drew hissed, leaning away as far as he could. "We're in a closet and there are men with guns out there." He moved as far away as he could, which wasn't far and put his back to the wall.

Puzzled by these contradictory statements, Williams moved closer and discovered why Drew was freaking out: the kid was hard as a rock under the flimsy chenille draperies. Never what anyone would call shy, Williams clamped one hand over Drew's mouth and wrapped the other around his erection.

After a token struggle, Drew moaned softly while Williams explored his crotch. Taking this for the surrender it was, Williams took his hand off Drew's mouth and replaced it with his lips as he stroked a harder part of Drew's anatomy. The young man tasted of wine, cake and something a little earthier and definitely female. This last made Williams tighten his grip and shove his tongue deeper into Drew's mouth. He was pleased when Drew responded by tilting his head for better access and undulating against Williams' hand. Williams had to clamp his hand back over Drew's mouth when he came and hold him until he stopped shaking. He wiped him down with the bedspread.

Neither of them had any idea how long the shooting had been going on downstairs, but it ended soon after Drew came down from his orgasm.

"What about you?" he asked in the sexiest breathy voice Williams had heard in days.

"I believe I'll wait a bit," Williams said, reaching

for his cell phone vibrating in his back pocket. He told his reliable contact's extraction squad leader where they were and not to shoot them when they came out.

There was so much glass and debris, not to mention blood and body parts, on the floor, that Williams slung Drew over his shoulder and carried him down to the car. "My hotel," Williams said in Russian, settling Drew on the seat next to him. "And tell your boss I owe him."

"He'll be pleased to hear that," the driver said and sped off at the front of the little convoy of unmarked cars, passing the police on their way back to the city center.

"Where are we going?" Drew asked. "My place is over in–"

"My hotel," Williams said. "The back entrance. You're not exactly dressed for the lobby."

"I have more clothes at my place," Drew said coolly.

"Oh, clothes– clothes are overrated," Williams murmured. He switched to Russian and told the driver to hurry.

Once in Williams' suite, Drew became distant, vague and rather cold. Williams offered him a drink; this was politely refused. "Is something wrong, Mr. Ryan?" Williams asked, keeping his distance, but staying between Drew and the door.

Drew laughed. "Oh, kind of," he said, sounding embarrassed. "After, um, everything tonight...I've, ah, forgotten your name."

"Reid, John Reid," Williams said, always glad to repeat one of his favorite aliases.

"Ah, yes, well, Mr. Reid, I–"

"John, Mr. Ryan, please call me John," Williams said, moving a little closer to the young man twisting the toga-like chenille bedspread in his hands.

"I will, John, please call me Drew..."

"Drew? Not Andrew or Andy?" Williams asked, very close to Drew's bare shoulder.

"Just Drew. Or Ryan," he said, turning and looking

him in the eye. "I answer to either."

"Drew," Williams sighed. "What can I do for you, Drew?"

"What are you doing here?" Drew asked.

"I'm thinking how lucky I am to have met you tonight."

"Oh, what a line," Drew said, rolling his eyes. "Now, for real, what are we doing here? You didn't just show up at, at whatever that place was."

"The whorehouse?" Williams paused to parcel out the truth and fiction he was going to tell Drew. "Not my kind of place usually. I was following the lady you spent the evening with."

"Why? I mean, why were you following her?" Drew asked, stepping away from Williams so he could pace. He turned and looked the older man in the eye. "Is she your wife?" he asked.

"No, no, not my wife. Not even my mistress. I believe she is a terrorist and has plans to attack the United States," Williams said blandly.

"By herself?" Drew asked.

"Ah, no," Williams laughed. "But I'm trying to find out who she's working with. Is it you?"

"No! I just met her this afternoon." Drew ran his hands through his hair. "I, fuck, it's confusing." He sat down at the table and ate a grape from the complimentary fruit basket.

"Hungry?" Williams asked, knowing people talked more when they were comfortable.

"A little," Drew admitted.

"Why don't you take a shower and relax?" Williams suggested. "I'll order a late supper for us. I'm hungry, too."

While Drew was in the shower, Williams ordered up a magnum of champagne to go with the tomato wedges, sliced cucumbers, Russian salad, shredded beet salad, caviar and smoked sturgeon. Shortly before this feast arrived, Drew emerged from the bathroom wearing one of the fluffy white robes the hotel provided. It was too big on him, which made it all the sexier.

They sat at the table and ate and drank in silence. Williams toasted Ryan's health.

"Thanks," Ryan said, moodily sipping his champagne. "I guess I still have it because of you. All that shooting...I wouldn't have known what to do..."

"Drop and roll for cover is the general rule," Williams said with a wry smile. Drew stared at him. "What were you doing there anyway?" Williams asked, casually, as if he was only making conversation and it didn't matter at all to him.

"Mademoiselle took me there," Drew said with a little laugh. "She came to my room this afternoon...seems like it was a long time ago..."

"Are you often visited by international terrorists?" Williams asked pleasantly.

"No! I hardly ever get visitors..." Drew gave Williams an appraising look over his champagne flute. "She brought me some money from Reagan. Then she took it and my laptop."

"Reagan?"

"Yeah, a gamer named Reagan in Electricland," Drew said, helping himself to more Russian salad and caviar.

Williams had a great poker face. Even so, his eyes widened at the name 'Electricland' and he fought down the turmoil inside him. "Electricland? What's that?" he asked innocently.

"Just an online game I play a lot," Drew said. He yawned and looked longingly at the bed.

"Tired?" Williams asked, taking the hint.

"Yes and no." Drew stood up, closed the distance between them, and leaned down to press his lips to Williams'. It was a clumsy kiss, but a very sweet one.

"Then I think we should lay down," Williams said, leading him to the big bed. "But not sleep."

"Mmmm, that sounds good," Drew sighed, slipping out of his robe and into bed. "But, first, do you have a laptop I can check my email on?"

"Sure." Williams handed the kid his brand new laptop and said he was going to take a shower. He felt confident the kid would be there when he got done because he could tell the kid was looking forward to more sex and he wouldn't get very far wearing only a bathrobe.

"So tell me about Electricland," Williams asked, sliding into bed next to Drew. The day was catching up with him, but the shower revived him. He played his fingertips over Drew's chest, peaking his nipples and getting a rewarding shudder for his trouble.

Drew leaned comfortably against Williams and told him about the game, his struggles with Reagan and the other players and his suspicions that there was something more going on than just gaming.

"How so?" Williams asked.

"The more challenging each level gets, the more boring the interface is," Drew said. "But then, when you win that level by breaking into whatever it is and sending the booty to Reagan, you get these lush screens again. It's weird."

"Show me," Williams ordered, making it sound like a request.

Drew opened a new tab and logged into Electricland.

In Titania's office in Maryland, Miranda murmured, "Ah, there you are Klaarance."

Next to her, Titania looked up from the classified DARPA data she was rifling through. "Wait, I want to know where Viola is." She woke the agent up and was satisfied she wasn't anywhere near the explosion.

Miranda cued the detonation sequence for the C4 in Klaarance's apartment. Klaarance stayed in the game. "This cannot be right," she said, as Klaarance kept trying to contact her Reagan avatar. "He cannot still be in the game."

"What's wrong?" Titania asked, leaning over her. She hated the game, but could see very clearly that

Klaarance was still running around in there.

"He's still alive," Miranda said.

"Maybe it didn't detonate," Titania told her and began to call Baku again so Viola could go look. Miranda's gasp stopped her.

"He's in our network!"

"Get him out!"

"I– I can't! I can't see where he is anymore." Miranda was frantically tapping keys. "I was tracing his location and then–"

Titania didn't hear the rest; she was running down the hall to hit the circuit breakers for that floor. She counted to ten, turned them back on and walked back into Miranda's office. "He better be gone now," she said.

"He is," Miranda said in a hollow voice.

"What did he get?"

"I don't know, but he did something he'd never done before."

"What?"

"He headed right for our financial records," Miranda said, looking up at her. "Like he knew what he was looking for."

"Where is he?" Titania asked coldly.

"I don't know which room, but he's at the Park Hyatt," Miranda said. "Viola's at the Grand Hotel, near it."

"Get back online, please, and get me the guest records," Titania said, tapping her foot until the names and room numbers started scrolling across her LCD. "There. John fucking Reid. It must be him."

"How do you know?" Miranda asked, pulling up the layout of the Park Hyatt.

"I know Williams. I know him well." Titania looked at her watch and called Viola in Baku.

In one of the best beds in the Park Hyatt, Drew was trying to log back into Electricland and getting nowhere. "I'm locked out," he said, shutting the laptop. "How did you know how to open those files? They weren't part of the game, not even game files."

"Oh..." Williams kissed Drew's neck. "I tried to play this game once, but I never had anyone as good as you to help me before."

"I–"

"Let's talk about it in the morning," Williams whispered against Drew's lips.

Viola felt pretty stupid slithering into the service entrance of the Park Hyatt and up the freight elevator to William's floor. All she really had was the element of surprise, if that. Williams was a cagey bastard; he might be waiting for her to do just this, if he knew she was in town. She pressed her new gun's silencer against the door lock and blew it open. Diving in, she fired twice at the bed and rolled into a crouch, ready for return fire. There wasn't any: the room as empty. They'd gone.

"Merde," Viola hissed on her way down the stairs as she called Titania. "Gone. And so am I."

"At least make sure Ryan's place blew up," Titania said. "We'll start looking for Williams. If he's with Ryan, they'll surface eventually."

Viola walked several blocks away from the hotel to shoot a cab driver and take his vehicle to Ryan's apartment building.

"Are you sure that's your building?" Williams asked Drew again. "Or rather, what's left of it?"

"Why...why would someone blow up my building?" Drew asked again.

"It's probably very complicated," Williams said patiently. He'd sent the cab driver into the café for tea, hoping a hot drink would snap Drew out of his funk.

"Do you know, I mean, who or why or, um..." The night was catching up with Drew and he wasn't making a lot of sense. Even to himself.

"No. Or possibly," Williams said, handing Drew

some tea and telling the driver to go back to the hotel. They'd just pulled up to the corner when another taxi shot at them. The driver was killed and the cab rolled across the intersection and into a building. Williams drew his pistol and shot at the other taxi as it sped away.

"What the fuck?! Who was that?" Drew was nearly hysterical.

"I didn't get a look at her," Williams said, helping Drew out of the crashed taxi and over to a working one.

"Her?" Drew stumbled in the too large slippers the hotel dug up for him. He was still only wearing the white terry cloth bathrobe.

"Him, it, something, anything," Williams murmured. He snarled in Russian and shoved enough money at the driver to get them very quickly away from a bad situation. There was no point in going back to the hotel, so he told the driver to take them to the train station where Williams bought two tickets for the next train going anywhere. Once settled into a compartment with Drew, he called his contact in Tbilisi. "Mademoiselle is here, possibly others. I've got a hot lead," he said, looking at Drew curled up in the corner of the seat. "But I need help getting him out."

The contact called him back ten minutes later with an address in the Old City. Williams dug up some clothes, shoes and a wifi connection for Drew while they waited. Two days later, they were taken by private plane to a landing strip outside of Ankara. A replacement passport was waiting for Drew at the American Embassy in the city.

By then Viola was in Tbilisi, not exactly waiting for Williams, but ready to kill him if he happened to show up. She knew he had a powerful contact in Tbilisi, so she assumed that's where he'd run to eventually. She was still annoyed that she'd missed him in Baku. Too many people around, even at that hour. She'd driven the damaged taxi as far as she could and then walked most of the way back to her hotel, where she'd calmly checked out and gone to the airport. While waiting for her flight, she called Titania. "Yes, it was Williams," she said. "And Ryan is with him. No, I have no idea why, but they're both dead men."

Chapter 8

Attorney Client Privilege

"Your people aren't very effective, Agent Titania," her Section Manager sneered at her.

"Not where Williams is concerned, no," she agreed. "That man is inhumanly lucky."

"So it would seem," the Department Manager murmured, looking at his notes. "But your group was very effective in Irvine."

"Yes, everything went as planned," Titania said with a sigh. "Until we had to cover our tracks at the DARPA installation. Then it got very untidy."

"So you telling us your first time with a guy was in a closet during a gunfight?" Bishop asked. "That's weird, man," he added when Drew nodded. "He didn't even screw you."

"He did later on," Drew said, with a smile. "While we were waiting for the plane, we were stuck in this house and there was nothing else to do."

"How was it?" Samsa asked.

Drew's eyes got dreamy. "Nice. He was very gentle. He–"

"Bishop! You have a visitor!" A correctional officer escorted him out of the cell and down the tier. Bishop had barely had a chance to shoot Samsa a warning glare before he was led away.

"You were saying?" Samsa asked, moving closer on the bunk.

"He was very gentle," Drew said, not moving away.

"Like this?" Samsa asked, kissing him deeply. He worked Drew's pants open and stroked him to hardness while Drew did the same for him.

Moving on top of the kid, Samsa humped their erections together until they came, Drew shooting slightly before his protector. "Mmmm, ya got no idea how long I wanted to do that," he whispered in Drew's ear. "It was so nice."

"Yeah," Drew said. "Hey, what's your first name?"

Samsa laughed and said, "Gregor."

"You're kidding." Drew sat up.

"No, not kidding."

They pulled their clothes back together just in time for Drew to be called to a visitor room.

Bishop found Russek waiting for him. "Your timing sucks, copper."

"Thanks, Bishop, this is the first chance I've had to get here," Russek said. "It's crazy out there."

"That's why I like it here so much," Bishop said. "What can I do for ya, Russek?"

"How's Drew?"

"He okay," Bishop said.

"And?"

"And? And? And what?" Bishop asked. "He's in jail, so far he ain't been gang raped in the showers or murdered or–"

"Bishop!"

"What? He fine. Even got a nice boyfriend," Bishop said coolly.

"WHAT!"

"Calm down," Bishop growled. "Some guy named Samsa helped us out. Guy is very well behaved and they very well chaperoned. Usually. Except when I'm not there, which is never, except for now."

Russek yelled for the guard to get Drew Ryan to an interview room.

On his way back to his cell, Bishop got called for another visitor. Well, not really a visitor: it was his lawyer, Kevin Orselli, Esquire.

"Oh, man, what you want, Kevin?" Bishop sighed on the other side of the bulletproof glass.

"Can't an attorney visit his client?" Orselli asked in his most cloying voice.

"I ain't seen you since you plea bargained me in here," Bishop said. "Thanks again for that. It crazy out there."

"Yes, very crazy." Orselli said, looking at his perfectly manicured nails. "One has to be so careful these days." He swept his dirty blond hair off his forehead. "Take Mr. Mitropolus, my former boss; very sad, his accident, completely unexpected." He paused for the question Bishop didn't ask. "His car blowing up that way, most unexpected, but not uncommon these days. Cars are blowing up all over the city."

"Really? Hey, I hope you not getting me out of here," Bishop said, glancing at the clock and then the guard and not getting any satisfaction from either of them. "I'm all nice and settled."

"Yes," Orselli sighed and smiled. His smile was disturbingly lewder than usual. "I understand you have a rather charming cellmate at the moment."

"How the fuck you know that, Kev?" Bishop stared hard at him.

"Our new boss, Mr. Lopez, seems very interested in Andrew Ryan's present accommodation," Orselli said, staring back with his fishy blue eyes.

"Why?" Bishop asked, creeped out as usual by Orselli's focused stare.

"I've no idea," Orselli said, smiling and going all vague and comfortable again. "I just got sent down here to make sure Ryan, and you, are okay and get you anything you might need. Is there any–?"

"No." Bishop decided to leave Russek's interest out. He was mulling over whether to tell Russek his creepy lawyer had an interest now. Or, his creepy lawyer's new boss, whoever the fuck that was. "We done?"

"Yes," Orselli said, rising gracefully. "You do know how to get in touch with me, don't you?" He listened to Bishop rattle off his cell phone number.

"Yes, that's it. Have a nice day, Luke."

Bishop hated the way Orselli said his first name, dragging it out and rolling it around in his slack mouth, so he got out of the room as quick as he could. He needed to check on Samsa, since he knew where Drew was.

Russek was pacing when Drew arrived in the interview room. "So, who's this Samsa guy?" he asked, ignoring Drew's welcoming smile, which promptly vanished.

"Just a guy," Drew said, with the awkward inmate sullenness he was nowhere near perfecting.

"Bishop says he's your boyfriend," Russek said and got laughed at. "It's not funny, Drew."

"He's not my boyfriend," Drew said, trying not to laugh. "He's just a guy I owe favors for keeping me safe in here."

"Isn't that what Bishop is doing?"

"It's crazy in here, Paul," Drew said, getting stressed. "We got jumped by a bunch of guys. Twice, once in the old jail and once in the new place. Both times Samsa bailed us out. Y'know, jacking him off is, like, the least I can do."

Russek was nonplussed, and then recovered. "I have got to get you out of here," he said hollowly.

"That would be good," Drew said softly.

Russek crossed the room and hugged him. The guard ignored them as they kissed.

"Look, about this Samsa guy," Russek said more kindly. "The jailhouse is not the place to be exploring your sexuality." He managed to keep a straight face as Drew smiled up at him.

"I'm not," Drew said softly. "I'm just doing the best I can."

"I'll get you out of here as soon as I can." Russek stepped back from him. "It's crazy in the city. Car bombs, freeway shootings, run away semi-trucks in Hollywood. There's so much, some of it's copycat stuff. A few witnesses said they saw old women doing the shooting."

"That's crazy," Drew said. "Gunslinger Grannies?"

"Yeah, totally crazy," Russek said. He nodded at the guard, who was pointing at his watch. "I left you some money at the cashier. I'll get you out of here as soon as I can. Stay safe with Bishop and this Samsa guy, I guess."

"Don't worry about it," Drew said.

"I have to worry," Russek said on his way out. "Bishop says the situation is under control."

"Then it is," Drew said, smiling. "Bye, Paul."

"Bye." Russek walked out of the jailhouse and back into a jumpy, stressed-out city.

"It's getting mighty dangerous out there," Isabella said with quiet satisfaction.

Helena looked up from the Calendar section of the Los Angeles Sunday Times. "Yeah, goddamn amazing what three dedicated women can accomplish on the ground."

"And presently we'll be four," Isabella said, checking her watch. "Kate should be back with Viola round 'bout now."

"We'll have to move to a bigger, swankier place," Helena said, tossing the paper in the corner of the motel room. "Viola can't stay in anything less than four stars."

"She's spoiled that way," Isabella agreed. "Wonder what she'll add to this mission. We really don't need her."

"Well, we always need her, honey, and we might need her here," Helena said. "I'm getting nowhere with Ryan at the jailhouse; maybe she can seduce some information out of him."

"Oh, I meant, you know..."

"Terrorism?" Helena asked and got a nod. "That's right, you've never worked an urban assault with her before. Viola's a lot like Kate; she trained Kate somewhere in the Middle East. She doesn't like to get her hands dirty, but likes to play with her victims for a while. Risky shit, but she's got something like nine hundred lives. Viola doesn't like being in the United States, so it's something special her coming here."

Isabella started to say something and then fell silent listening to a car pulling up. "I hope that's them," she said, reaching for her gun. "They're late."

Helena picked up a copy of Sunset Magazine to cover her gun and waited tensely for the door to open. "Well, well," she said, smiling sarcastically. "If it ain't the child molester come to visit."

"Helena!" Kate looked scandalized.

"Oh, Helena, hello to you, too, darling, and do shut up," Viola snarled urbanely. "I have jet-lag and the flight from JFK to LAX was barbaric." She looked around the room. "Dear God, how long have you been living in this squalor?" she asked, swaying slightly.

"Bless your little heart, Viola," Isabella drawled. "Well, I like it. It's right homey." She poured Viola some brandy in a Styrofoam cup.

Viola raised an eyebrow at the cup, but downed the booze. "Ah, that's better. I apologize for my rudeness," she said wearily. "I just need a nap, a shower, some good food, fine wines, and all of those in the nice hotel we're moving to. And maybe a nice young man later on."

"Pervert," Helena said good-naturedly as she gathered up her meager luggage.

"Maybe, but I only want him for sex," Viola said holding the door for her and Isabella. "It's love that perverts even the whitest soul."

"Golly, how philosophical," Isabella said blandly. "I hope it's a big suite so I don't have to listen to you and some stud all night."

"I'll get some earplugs for you, Isabella, if you need them," Kate said, with a laugh in her voice as she wedged their bags into the rented Mercedes trunk that was already full of Viola's luggage.

Isabella drove, Kate next to her, and Helena and

Viola in the backseat.

"Here," Helena said, handing Viola a Kahr PM9 pistol and Scorpion silencer. "Titania said you liked this gun in Baku."

"How thoughtful of her," Viola said, checking her new gun out. She'd thrown the old one out of the taxi on the way to the Baku international airport. "I do like this gun. Have you tried it?"

"I did a little shooting with it last night in Santa Monica," Helena said. "Close range stuff, some of it in noisy, party crowds. Nobody seems to notice. And if anyone does notice, they just think the person was drunk and a nice old lady was helping them lay down. It's a good gun for that."

Viola studied her for a moment. "Are they really that stupid here?" she asked.

"They're a strange combination of callous and stupid," Isabella said, only turning slightly away from the road before her. "At least the drunken party crowds are."

"I'm surprised there isn't a curfew and patrols," Viola said casually.

"Have you noticed the size of this place?" Helena asked. "You'd need an army to enforce a curfew and patrol this nuthouse."

"Can't keep people from their fun, luv," Kate said. "You'd think the population would know to get off the streets with all the drive-bys, freeway shootings and explosions lately. And not all by us: we've got copycats."

"The most sincerest form of flattery," Isabella said. "And very helpful; we can't be everywhere."

"Even if it seems like it," Kate said. "Miranda says the local press and blogs are abuzz with tales of the Menopausal Terrorists."

"Menopausal Terrorists!" Viola laughed, clapping her hands. "Oh, la la! That's too funny!"

"Parts of the city are off the streets at night," Helena said. "The poorer, working class parts, but they're not usually in clubs at three AM. They got more sense than that."

"Well then, let's leave them alone. They're not the sort of people the world notices dying anyway, so no reason to waste our time on them," Viola said. "I understand there's some very nice shopping near our hotel. I believe it's called Rodeo Drive. Let's blow some of it up over the next few days, shall we?"

Los Angeles began to experience a series of robberies, shootings, and bombings at luxury goods stores. The police could discern no pattern: one day it was an expensive boutique in Beverly Hills, another day it was a Ferrari dealership down the street. The incidents moved from Hollywood to Brentwood to Santa Monica and back again. There was no rhyme or reason to the attacks, and the randomness frayed the city's nerves even further. The only lead the police had were a few strange reports of middle-aged women near the targets. The successful targets, that is; there were other incidents, mostly by men in the Valleys and at Marina del Rey, who merely blew themselves up or got caught. The ones the police couldn't catch were women of a certain age, women who left such a vague impression, they were almost ghosts. Or women so elegant and gracious that, if they could be found, they could hardly be considered suspects.

The LAPD's desperate response to all this was to start rounding up all the middle-aged women they could find. Mothers, daughters, aunts, sisters, grandmothers, wives, spinsters, friends, co-workers, many of whom had never even had a traffic ticket were swept off the streets and into custody. The jails began to groan under the strain; dormitories, hospitals, and hotels were commandeered as "holding centers" into which suspects were processed after their threat level was assessed at the local precincts or the Women's Jail in Lynwood. The people of Los Angeles began to grow angry with the police; more angry than afraid.

Even the LAPD was nervous at the state the city was in. When wildfires rage out of control in Southern California, extra firefighters are called in from other counties, other states and even other countries. The LAPD had no such resources to fall back on. They only had overtime, lots of it, which made for a lot of tired, trigger-happy cops on the streets. Cops were even accidentally shooting each other. It was nuts, very nuts. Russek was repeatedly told to be more careful than usual. Working double shifts, he was as exhausted as his fellow officers. All he could do when he got home was fall into bed and get a few hours of dreamless sleep. He had no time to check on Drew; he could only hope the kid was okay in the slammer with Bishop. It was probably the safest place to be just then.

Drew was having problems of his own. His new jail was overflowing again with guys on terrorism charges. There were two more in their cell. Even if he wasn't enjoying sleeping in Bishop's arms every night, there was nowhere else for him to safely sleep. Samsa was also looking a little stressed. At least Drew could let off a little steam in his therapy sessions with Dr. Smith, whom he was starting to like.

Drew: "I know I've only been in this jail for a month, but it feels like forever. My life before here seems like a dream. I know I came here with one guy, and then I fell in love with another guy, but I'm almost happy in here. I feel safe in a strange way."

Smith: "Hmmm."

Drew: "Even though the food is bad and there's nothing to do and there are four men in a two man cell, outside there's just crime, traffic and not enough money. That was always my problem: money. I never had enough, I always wanted more, more, more. In here, there's no money and all my needs are taken care of. So, what, really, am I missing out there?"

Smith: "How about the internet?"

Drew: "Oh...the internet, yes, I do miss that."

Smith: "What about it do you miss?"

Drew: "Well, there was this game I liked to play on it."

"You know Helena's not getting anywhere with Drew," Isabella said, driving away from their ammo depot at the Secure Borders Project. She'd taken Viola to pick out some new guns and stock up on C4; they were running low.

"I can imagine she isn't," Viola said. "There isn't anywhere to get with him. I was just glad I only had to kill him."

"And have sex with him," Isabella added.

"At least I succeeded at that," Viola said with some bitterness. "I still don't know how he ended up with Williams, but there he was."

"Yes, ma'am, there they were," Isabella said. "Williams and Drew, and Drew hacking into Miranda's files through Electricland with Williams' help."

"Ouf, that fucking game!" Viola spat. "I despise the internet."

"I don't nearly understand what Miranda does, but it's usually useful," Isabella said. She was learning a lot and really enjoying working with Viola. The older woman was so direct and elegant in her ideas about how to get the maximum panic with the minimum risk and effort. And there was always a kind of flair to it, too.

"How?" Viola asked, inspecting the Glock she'd picked up.

"Oh, planting rumors, moving money around, gathering information."

"So that little beast Ryan can steal it for Williams?" Viola asked, rhetorically since Isabella didn't have an answer. "Oh, perhaps I'm being unfair. I like things when they work and this internet thing usually worked, but that disaster at DARPA was a...a..."

"Disaster?" Isabella helpfully suggested.

"Yes, and a bad one, too."

Isabella merged onto the freeway. "Where we headed, Miss Viola? It's purt nigh time to got rid of this vehicle."

"It's what?" Viola asked.

"We've had this car long enough," Isabella clarified. They'd carjacked the Jaguar at the Pacific Design Center parking lot and they'd have to get rid of it fairly soon before the former owner began to smell up the trunk. Viola had the marvelous idea of wiring the trunk to blow as soon as someone opened it to find out what the dreadful smell in it was. Brilliant! Simply brilliant!

"Some large parking structure somewhere," Viola said. "We'll stick these plates on whatever we steal. I have some ideas for gasoline."

"Like what?" Isabella asked, delighted.

"Oh, mainly arson, but I'd like to find some hills with cars parked on them," Viola said, waving her hands around. "I'd like to pour the gasoline down the hill, under the cars and set it on fire. We'll have get away fairly quickly, or do it in a crowded area where we can blend in. Possibly use more fire as a diversion to get away. I'll need to look at some potential targets before we do anything. Too bad the hills are so green this time of year. Wildfires would be excellent here now."

"Oh yes, that would panic 'em! Los Angeles has those hills around it that burn like crazy. Too bad it's so early in the year."

"Yes, it's a pity."

"Are you off C4?" Isabella asked with a note of disappointment in her voice. "We are going to wire this car up before we burn the place down, aren't we?"

"Oh, yes, of course, my dear," Viola assured her. "But we've done that trick about half a dozen times now, sooner or later the bomb squad is going to get wise."

"Yessum, I bet they'd bring those bomb sniffing dogs," Isabella said, reasonably.

"I wonder if those dogs can smell C4 over the smell of rotting human." Viola slid a clip into her new Glock and put it in her purse. "I don't know if they can. Do you know?"

Isabella shook her head and pointed the car toward Century City.

In Titania's offices in Maryland, Miranda was reading some very angry message boards in Los Angeles. The crack-down on terrorism was stirring up tremendous amounts of online rage, much of it in Spanish, which Miranda used an online translator to understand as her Spanish was very weak. Some of it she showed to Titania, who was able to post misdirection and rumor on the boards in that language.

"Who's Maria Martinez, coming up from Juarez?" Miranda asked, puzzling her way through one of Titania's Spanish message board posts.

"No one," Titania said. She was logging into one of the new secure accounts they'd set up to replace the ones Ryan and Williams stole. They'd still need to know exactly what Ryan had gotten that night at DARPA. Kate had gotten into Russek's love nest as his housekeeper and uploaded the contents of Ryan's laptop to Miranda's server. But, however perversely interesting the contents of that machine were, the information they were after was not on it.

"Yet you write here that she's coming to Los Angeles to lead the rebellion," Miranda said. She was slightly distracted by Hermia moving a large amount of money into one of their secure accounts. Things were moving in South and Central Asia again, which was good in case their oil sheiks decided to stop funding their anti-terrorism accounts. This seemed unlikely due to the fact that Los Angeles had become a terrorism magnet and America's anti-terrorism organizations needed all the help they could get. The sheiks were very generous and it wasn't very hard to keep secret the fact that at least fifteen of the organizations they were funding were all run by Titania's group under various fronts.

"It's a lie," Titania said, looking over the accounts

with a small smile. Things were getting back in order, Ryan was the only loose end, and they'd tie him off as soon as he was out of jail. "When is Ryan getting out of jail?"

"I'm checking," Miranda said, searching the LA court records for Ryan's name. "Won't they be disappointed when she doesn't show up?"

"When who doesn't show up?" Titania asked. She was doing a quick reconciliation of one of the more active accounts.

"When Maria Martinez doesn't show up," Miranda said, sorting and scanning her records.

"Yes."

"Titania!"

Titania blew out a breath. "Give them hope and take it away," she said. "You then have very, very angry people. People capable of violence." She looked at her watch and stood up. "What about Ryan?"

"Still checking," Miranda said. "If you're going to do a false messiah for the Latinos, what about for the Blacks? The LAPD is oppressing them, too."

"I'll think about it," Titania said, wearily. "All I can think about right now is Ryan. Ryan? You remember Ryan, don't you, Miranda?"

"Yes. There's nothing in the Courts or Police about releasing him," Miranda said. "Why don't we plant the idea he'd lead them to the source of all the violence in LA?"

"Because he might just do that," Titania said, thoughtfully. "Plant the idea where?"

"DHS, FBI, DOD, C-"

"DOD."

Miranda looked up at her boss, who was smiling again.

"Ah. Yes. The Department of Defense," Titania mused. "Yes. If DARPA thought Ryan could lead them to whoever broke into their system, they'd spring him in a heartbeat, wouldn't they?"

Miranda nodded.

"Plant some seeds, Miranda," Titania said. "Let's see what sprouts."

Kate went to see her Samoan gang girls. They were glad to see her, or rather, they were glad to see her money again. They had a new leader, a girl named Pika.

"When?" she asked.

"I don't know," Kate said. "It will be like last time, I'll let you know when as soon as I know."

"Where?" Pika asked, looking appropriately suspicious.

"I don't know that either," Kate told her. "Yet. I have your mobile number, I'll ring you up."

"Money?" Pika seemed more interested.

"Same as last time," Kate said.

"It's more this time," Pika said. She stood up and looked menacingly down at Kate.

Kate took her suppressed Mauser out of her purse and shot her in the chest and then, just to make sure, she shot her in the head. "So, who's the leader now?" she asked the survivors.

After a few seconds, a girl named Sina stepped forward and the negotiations were swiftly concluded. As she drove away, Kate tossed the Mauser, but not the suppressor, out of the car window. If one of those girls wanted it, they were certainly welcome to it.

Over high tea at the Biltmore, Viola asked her if she trusted them.

"Enough for one more operation," Kate said between bites of caviar sandwich.

"Won't they be angry you've killed one of their own?" Viola asked pleasantly. They were speaking French and kept the tone chatty and casual. "Don't they have *esprit de corps* or a code of honor or something like that?"

"They're realists," Kate said. "That girl died because she was stupid and too greedy. The other girls want to succeed and now they know how to do it." She sipped at her tea; they served a decent Ceylon at the

Biltmore. "I did give them more money."

"Oh? That seems like a sign of weakness," Viola observed.

"Not when I explained that either they could bring in another girl for the job or they could divide the late Pika's share amongst themselves," Kate said with a smile. "They seemed to appreciate that."

"Ah." Viola smiled back at her and flagged down a waiter for the check. The Biltmore was such a lovely place; she decided to keep it off the list of targets. It was too far east to be a serious target anyway. She'd just finished paying the bill when Isabella called Kate to tell her she was being arrested in a round up at the Beverly Center.

Chapter 9

To the Barricades

"Barbarians." Titania's Section Manager was right for once.

"Yes, arresting groups of middle-aged women in overpriced climate-controlled cavernous shopping malls on a lovely spring day is, indeed, barbaric," Titania agreed.

"I've only read the newspaper accounts and some wild DHS speculation on the incident," the Department Manager said. "What did you do about it?"

"Well," Titania said, smoothing her skirt. "I did the best I could."

"Oh shit," was all Miranda could say when Titania rushed into her computer room to tell her Isabella was in custody in Los Angeles.

"She won't talk," Titania said. "Fire up your machines and find her. What name is she using?"

"Mary Anne Evans."

"Why do I know that name?" Titania massaged her temples.

"It's George Eliot's real name."

"Ah, the novelist." Titania smiled briefly at Miranda's nod. "Hm. How nice, how literary. Where is she?"

"George Eliot is dead, but it looks like the LAPD is sending Isabella for processing at the King/Drew hospital," Miranda said.

"Where's Helena?" Titania asked, logging onto her LA message boards and favorite revolutionary blogs.

"Awaiting instructions," Miranda said. "As are Viola and Kate."

"Put an order into the LAPD system that Mary Anne Evans is to have a psych intake with Dr. Linda Smith at this King/Drew place before she's booked and put into incarceration." Titania never stopped typing as she said this. "It is Linda Smith, right? A somewhat normal name."

Miranda said, "Yes," over her own typing.

"Tell Kate and Viola to get lots of guns and go down to the Lynwood Women's Jail," Titania said, still typing like mad. "Tell them to put the guns in bags and hand them out and then get out as quickly as possible. There's going to be a riot, and it should be a very violent riot, so all the police in LA County go there to subdue it."

"Viola wants to know why there's going to be a riot," Miranda relayed, phone jammed against her ear.

"Because the famous Latina revolutionary, Maria Martinez, is being held incognito at the Lynwood Jail," Titania said, still typing furiously. "And she needs to be rescued."

After a quick stop at the Secure Borders Project ammo dump, Kate drove them quickly down to Lynwood. Threading their way through the rapidly expanding multicultural crowd in front of the jail, they casually left bags of guns in their wake. One or two kind souls called them back to tell them they'd left their bag, which was very nice, but slowed the gun distribution down.

"They have guns. Why aren't they shooting the police?" Viola asked irritably.

"Los Angeles," Kate sighed. "It's a bloody mystery."

"Well, fuck it." Viola got out of the car and took a plastic bottle out of the trunk. She asked Kate to point the car away from the spontaneous but orderly assembly. She accosted a man waiting at a red light and shot him when he rolled his window down. "It's all right," she said to the woman in the car behind his.

"He's just passed out." Shoving his body over to the passenger side, she poured the bottle of gasoline on the floor of the passenger side, lit it and rolled the flaming car into the well-mannered demonstration. It exploded and so did the riot.

"That's done it," Kate said, easing away from the curb. "Good work."

"Thank you. Slow down, please." Viola leaned across her to shoot the woman who'd been in the car behind the one that was now a burning wreck slammed into the Women's Jail. "She got a pretty good look at me."

"Yes, I'm sure she'd be able to recognize that dowdy head scarf anywhere," Kate said, driving past several police cars and vans screaming to the riot. "I hope Titania knows what she's doing."

"I'm certain she does. My dear, she arranged a riot in Los Angeles from her office on the other side of the country," Viola said with some awe in her voice. "I salute her."

But then they were called to the King/Drew hospital to create another diversion as there was another riot in progress there.

"Mon Dieu, cheri," Viola said as they skirted the edges of the escalating melee. "These people riot more than the French."

Isabella had a few quiet moments to think things over while she was being transported around Los Angeles. Since she couldn't escape, she escaped into reverie.

She never knew why she went down into the violence to rescue the woman the police were beating. By the time she got down there, the police had left her for dead, but she wasn't. She was, however, very heavy to drag/carry up the stairs to her SRO room.

Isabella, before she became Isabella, was very timid and always afraid. The riot that year in her Atlanta slum had kept her inside for days. She was as afraid of the rioters as she was of the police and rightly so. She'd watched the three policemen beat one woman to the ground, and something snapped inside her hungry, frightened body.

She cleaned up the woman's wounds as best she could and waited for her to wake up. It took the injured woman two days to come to. During those days, the police searched the buildings, looking for the dangerous terrorist they said had started the riots. Isabella, as she would later be called, hid the unconscious woman under her bed and acted crazy and drunk when they came to search her room. She was so scared, she peed on one of the officer's boots, and this made them go away a little quicker.

One night Isabella woke up because the woman was moaning and moving around, more than she had before. Then she opened her eyes.

"Jesus Christ," the woman sighed.

"I don't believe in him anymore," Isabella said primly.

"Just a figure of speech," the woman said, rubbing her neck. "Shee-yit. Am I still in Atlanta? Got some any aspirin or Advil or something?"

"Yes and yes." Isabella got up and rummaged around her medicine cabinet.

"Was there a purse with me?" the woman asked.

"No."

"Damn."

Isabella hovered until the woman noticed she was holding a cup and a generic aspirin bottle over her.

"Thanks," the woman said, taking the pills and asking for more water. "How did I get here and how long have I been here?"

"I brought you up," Isabella said. "You've been here for two, purt near three, days."

"Oh, Christ." She held up her hand. "Sorry. Oh, Elvis."

"Who are you?" Isabella asked.

"No one."

"The police were here. They're looking for

someone, " Isabella said. "If it's you, I think you should go."

Taking a look around the grim little room, the woman said, "They were in this room and didn't see me? The APD must be stupider than I thought."

"I– I hid you."

The woman gave her a long look. "Why?" she asked.

"There were three of them– policemen, three of them, beating on you with their sticks and kicking you while you were on the ground–" Isabella took several breaths, but still couldn't keep from crying. "That wasn't right, no matter what, it wasn't right. They do that all the time, gang up on a woman, beat her down, keep her down, kill her, crush her. I couldn't stand it. I just couldn't stand it!"

"Now, now, honey," the woman reached out and patted her rescuer's arm. "It was me they were beatin' on." This elicited a sniffly laugh. "So, did little you go down there and kill three policemens with your bare hands?"

"No, I–" Isabella lowered her head. "They were gone when I got there. I just brought you inside."

"That was lucky for me," the woman said softly. "You're a hundred percent right that I should go, but the sun's coming up. D'you mind if I stick around until dark?"

"I don't mind," Isabella said. "I got some food while you were asleep. Do you want a sandwich or some soup?" She bustled around her little room, offering this wounded woman what little hospitality she had.

Between naps and snacks, the woman listened to her savior's hard luck story. The woman who would become Isabella had been raised a traditional Christian Southern woman and married a traditional Christian Southern man who ignored her after their second child was born. Two more children later, and he began to beat her up. She appealed to their church and was told she must be obedient to her husband. She was; it made no difference in the weight of his blows. Praying didn't make her feel better. It made her feel more helpless. The more she prayed, the more things stayed the same in her hellish marriage. Then one day her husband got drunk and crashed the car with all her four children in it. Her family had been avoiding her and her bad marriage for years. Her church offered her empty words of condolence and then tried not to see her sitting there on Sundays. She ran out of money and lost the house. By then she was wandering the streets of her town, looking for her lost children. The good Christian townspeople's solution was to drive her up to the mean streets of Atlanta and drop her off at the first homeless shelter they came to. She'd gotten back on her feet enough to get General Assistance and a little SRO room to cower in. Saving an unconscious woman from being trampled in the riot was the bravest thing she'd done in years, maybe ever.

"My, my, that's the longest I've talked to someone in a long time," Isabella said, slightly hoarse.

"Damn, that's a tough story," the woman said quietly.

"I just thought–" She started to cry again. "I just thought that if I did what everyone told me to do, everything would be all right. And then it wasn't. Get married, go to church, have kids, trust in Jesus...and where was Jesus when I needed him?" She looked furiously at the woman sitting next to her.

"Tennessee?" the woman suggested.

"No! He was nowhere! That's why I don't believe in him anymore," she said, calming down a little. "That's when I didn't care about anything anymore."

"You cared about me," the woman said. "To go down there into that mess and get me."

"No...no, I got angry," Isabella said, almost to herself. "I got so angry watching them beating you. If I'd had a gun...or a knife...I don't know what I would have done."

The woman put her arm around her and Isabella leaned into her demi-embrace. "Don't squeeze me, honey, I think I've got a few cracked ribs."

They sat together until the sun was completely down and the street was quiet.

"I'm going to have to go now." She got unsteadily to her feet. "I don't believe in God, so I won't say God bless you, but I wish I could. So I'll just say thank you for my life."

Two weeks later, the woman, wearing an Anne Klein pantsuit and sensible shoes, returned to Isabella's SRO building in a limousine and took her away in it.

"But where are we going?" Isabella asked.

"Well, shee-yit, honey, anything's got to be better than where you were," the woman told her.

"At least tell me your name," Isabella demanded.

"Oh, just call me Helena."

The mob around King/Drew were chanting, "Free Lina Mott! Free Lina Mott!" at the riot squad.

"Who's Lina Mott?" Kate asked, watching more patrol cars and police vans roll in.

"I don't know." Viola was looking on impassively.

"Shouldn't we do something?" Kate asked, surprised by this passivity in the usually more aggressive Viola.

"Like what?" Viola asked, glancing up at the two helicopters nearly crashing overhead. "Find a bridge to get under?"

"I'm ringing Titania." Kate snapped her cell phone open.

"As you please, my dear," Viola said, watching the LAPD fail to menace the angry crowd.

"Did you do this one, too?" Miranda asked, gesturing at the television screen.

"No, the point of mine was to get the police away from there," Titania said irritably. "Not bring them in en masse."

"Who's Lina Mott?" Miranda asked, typing furiously.

"Nobody I invented," Titania murmured as she leaned over her keyboard, searching the internet for another diversion, if one could be drummed up. It seemed like everyone in the city was already in the streets.

"She's a...a, either a city council member from Denton, Texas, a chiropractor in Bloomington, Indiana, or an Army reservist with a blog between tours in Iraq," Miranda said.

"Which one is locked up in Drew/King?" Titania asked, picking up her phone.

"Um...the soldier, I think."

Titania looked over at Miranda and said, "Hmmm." Then she said hello to Kate. "Yes, Kate, we're watching it on TV....She's an Army reservist....no, I don't know what she's doing in there, probably just got grabbed in the sweep like Isabella....Have you seen Isabella or Helena yet?...No? Oh, too bad. What?...Do? What should you do?" Titania glanced at the television. "Do nothing. This riot seems to be coalescing on its own...No, no, I think two middle-aged women handing out Molotov cocktails would be a little suspicious...Just sit tight until you see Helena and Isabella and then get them out of there...Yes, yes...no, no, what kind of arms do you have on hand?" She listened as Kate read off her list. "All good, yes, guns, knives, machine guns, C4, and a what?...A bazooka? Really? That might be very handy. Yes, I leave it to you. Sorry, Kate, my other phone is ringing. Good luck."

Inside King/Drew, Isabella was getting a mite bored and thinking she really should do something about being locked up in a treatment room. Picking the lock to get out seemed like a good way to get shot and it was a long drop into a big riot from the window. She was just deciding her hips would not fit into the air conditioning shaft when the door opened and a guard ushered Helena in.

"Excuse me," Helena said, neatly stepping behind the guard and breaking his neck. "Get into these clothes," she told Isabella.

"I knew someone would come. I was hoping it'd be you," Isabella said, changing clothes with the dead guard. "Now what?" she asked, checking the guard's gun clip.

"Well, I don't know if we should wait for the mob down there to tear the place apart or see what the others are up to," Helena said, dialing her cell phone. "They are supposed to be out there backing us up."

"Well, I'm sure they are," Isabella said reasonably.

"Yeah, maybe," Helena said. "Knowing them, they might have gone shopping or something... Oh, hello, T, listen, I'm with I, can you get us out of here?...We're on the third floor over the main entrance....A stairwell?" She looked the question at Isabella, who told her she'd seen one across the hall, a few doors down. Helena relayed this information to Titania. "Yeah, some kind of a diversion would be great, thanks. What kind of diversion will it be?...I'll know it when see it? Well, okay, we'll starting making our way out the back, yes, thanks. Talk to you later." She snapped her phone closed and turned to Isabella. "Help me get this guard on the table and cover him up in case someone comes in."

There was so much turmoil in the hall, no one asked them where they were going. They were on the ground floor, heading for the back of the building when the first blasts hit the far end of the hospital.

"Dang, that's fast work," Isabella said.

Helena had no answer as they were both caught up in the wave of bodies trying to get away from the next blast. They were almost carried out of the building into the loading bays as the rioters rushed the police and swarmed into the burning building.

Kate and Viola left the bazooka in the cab of the semitruck they'd truck-jacked and headed back to their car. They'd gotten a few curious looks as they climbed out of the truck, but no one made a move to stop them. Just for good measure they blew the truck up, which would hopefully take care of anyone who could describe them. They'd put on scarves and wiped off all their make-up before they grabbed the truck that was stuck in traffic across from the hospital.

"I knew that bazooka was going to come in handy," Viola said, significantly more cheerful than before. She pulled the visor down and got out her lipstick.

"Yes, I'm so glad you insisted. I only wish they made a lighter bazooka. My back is going to hurt tomorrow," Kate said, getting behind the wheel. "Now how do we find Helena and Isabella?"

"We can call them and meet somewhere," Viola said, finishing her lips. "If they made it out of the building, that is."

"I certainly hope they did," Kate said. There were a lot of police around, so she decided to forego her own maquillage and get them out of there.

"Ah." Viola opened her ringing cell phone and relayed Helena's directions to a taco stand several streets southeast.

Later in the day, the Governor ordered the National Guard into the streets of Los Angeles to restore and maintain order. Due to the scarcity of Guardsmen, Marines were brought up from Camp Pendleton as well.

"Personally, Titania, I think the Governor is overacting and overreacting," Helena said from the nice hotel room they'd gotten in Pomona. "This situation is nothing the LAPD wasn't handling."

"Be that as it may," Titania said through clenched teeth. "Car bombs, bazooka attacks, exploding semi-trucks and city-wide riots have brought in the National Guard and the Marines, so I suggest you all get out of town for a while."

"You mean you don't want us to take on the National Guard and the Jarheads?" Helena asked, winking at Kate.

"No! No! For God's sake, no!" Titania yelled loud enough for the other women to hear her. "At this rate, there'll be tanks in the streets of Hollywood. Just go rest somewhere, somewhere nice, like Palm Springs or Las Vegas. And stay out of trouble until things calm down in LA." She hung up.

"I think the menopause is kicking Titania's ass," Helena said, relaying the last of the conversation to her audience of three.

"I think the car and truck bombs were a little much," Isabella said. "I think that's what really panicked them."

"But that was our intention, luv," Kate said briskly. "Panic and terror are very closely related. And the car wasn't a bomb, it was just on fire."

"And rolled into a crowd of people," Helena added. "Very effective, maybe too effective."

"Bollocks," Kate said, and looked pointedly at Isabella. "Remember why we were doing all this."

"Bless your little heart, Miss Kate. You know I'd do the same for any of y'all," Isabella said with hauteur.

"Oh, absolutely!" Kate said. "I–"

"Oh, Palm Springs," Viola cooed. "I've heard of that, let's go there, shall we? We'll have a nice long rest because it looks like the city isn't going to calm down very quickly."

"Sounds nice, darlin', but I'm going back to the city," Isabella said.

"Careful, Isabella," Kate warned. "They'll still be picking up middle-aged women."

"Especially ones that lookin' like they got car bomb fetishes," Helena murmured and got a sharp look from Viola.

"They won't be looking for a bag lady burn-out," Isabella said.

"Possibly, but still dangerous," Viola said. "Brava on initiative, though."

"I know this play," Helena said. "I'll go with you."

She held up her hand to forestall Kate and Viola's arguments. "The cops will be looking for nice middle-aged, middle class ladies. We'll be down in the mud, looking up. Well, Isabella will be. I can't do that bag lady thing; it gives me the heebie-jeebies. But I'll be somewhere nearby."

Viola looked from one American to the other while Kate looked at her. "You're fools," she finally said. "But I can see there's no way to talk you out of it. You know how to find us if you need us."

"Well, we always need you, Viola," Isabella drawled sweetly.

"You're also responsible for explaining why you didn't follow Titania's orders, if she asks," Viola said with equal sweetness. "Good luck."

"I'm sure she'll forgive us," Helena said. "We'll stay here until things cool down a little more."

They divided up what was left of the weapons and explosives before Kate and Viola left in the car. After a little discussion, Helena and Isabella decided they did need a little break. They rented a car, visited Joshua Tree and Desert Hot Springs, and headed back into the subdued chaos of Los Angeles a week later.

Chapter 10

Sprung in late Spring

"As you are aware, Agent Titania, the subsequent occupation of Los Angeles city and county are the primary reasons for this disciplinary committee meeting." The Department Manager massaged the bridge of his nose and consulted his notes while her more direct supervisor, the Section Manager, sat fuming beside him. "Can you explain to me how your four agents managed to pull apart the entire civil structure of the second largest city in the country?"

"This is what we do, sir," she said. "And we're very good at what we do."

"Possibly too good at it," he murmured.

"Four! Four! Four!" the Section Manager chanted. "There were only four of your agents in place. How could four agents do that much damage in a few weeks?"

"We usually don't have that many in place at one time," Titania said patiently. "It was necessary to keep the city off balance while we recovered Ryan's information. One agent could have done that; multiply it by three, and then four, and possibly this was more activity than the city was able to absorb." She looked from one man to the other. "The Los Angeles Police are also a rather tightly wound operation."

"What do you mean?" the Department Manager asked.

"We suspected, going in, that the LAPD had an overly aggressive, borderline paranoid, bloated middle management structure," Titania said. "We hypothesized that if we pushed on certain weaknesses, i.e., negative publicity from high-profile failures in the wealthy parts of the city, they'd panic and overreact to the stimulus. As you can see from the media reports, this is exactly what happened, albeit more than we anticipated."

"Yes, and it's become more and more obvious that the National Guard and Marines were called in to pull the heavily armed Los Angeles police force off the citizens who were, in many cases, equally heavily armed, and were fighting back with everything they had," the Department Manager said coldly. "And this is what my superiors are very concerned about."

"Yes," the Section Manager said firmly. "And how can we avoid such horrors in future?"

"We're not really interested in avoiding these things," the Department Manager said. "My superiors are more interested in how we can orchestrate them more efficiently."

Titania sat back and relaxed her shoulders. "Oh, I see," she said, folding her hands in her lap. "I'd have to look at my notes for that."

"You came here to die, didn't you?" the woman asked.

"I'm wearing dynamite strapped around my waist, so, yes, I came here to die," the other woman said.

"And you speak English," the woman observed.

"Very deductive, since you addressed me in that language and I responded in it," the other woman answered. "I say, you're not in charge of anything important, are you?"

"No."

"Good."

"However, you can take off the pack, we won't be needing you to blow yourself up today," the woman who would become Viola told the woman who would become Kate.

"But–"

"Oh, you'll be able to commit suicide," Viola said. "But you'll get to kill a lot of people and do a lot of damage before you do."

Kate glanced nervously at the large Syrian male

who was eavesdropping on their conversation as well as a non-Western language speaker could. "You know you seem a bit loony," she said in just above a whisper. "But this is the most interesting conversation I've had since I got here, so I'll go along with you."

"Good. Where are you from?"

"Baghdad. Or what's left of it."

"Ah," Viola said, bowing her head. "I understand."

"I bloody doubt it, luv."

Viola's cell phone ringing made Kate open her eyes and look over at her in the next mud bath. She pushed the cucumbers off her eyes in time to see Viola gingerly handling her phone with muddy fingers.

"Yes, yes, no, no, yes," Viola was saying. "Tomorrow at eleven? Good to know. Does he know? No? Good. Good-bye." She looked over at Kate. "Ryan is being released at eleven tomorrow. Titania thinks you should pick him up. I agree with this. See if you can get anything out of him."

"Well, it was a nice couple of weeks, wasn't it?" Kate asked. "I hope Isabella and Helena had nice weeks. What do you think of Isabella?"

"A charming lady," Viola said sincerely. "I'm so looking forward to working with her in the future. She is the master of disguise the way she blends into the milieu."

"Oh?" Kate asked, recalling Isabella's brilliant performance at the Secure Borders ammo dump.

"Yes, she claims this is because middle-aged women are invisible, especially to waiters and sales clerks," Viola said, relaxing back into her mud bath. "But I feel sure it's Isabella's innate ability to efface herself in a crowd. Brilliant, I wish I could do it."

"You have done it," Kate said. "I've seen you do it."

"Well, then I wish I could enjoy doing it as much as Isabella does."

In Los Angeles, Isabella was having little trouble

blending in on the deserted streets. At night she easily found a bed in one of the many makeshift shelters for displaced persons. By day she pushed her shopping cart around and around the Twin Towers jail, hoping to see something of interest. She looked like such a harmless old woman, she'd even made a few friends in the area. Shopkeepers, cops, jail guards, and employees all saved their cans and bottles for her. They, as well as Marines and Guardspersons, were kind to her. It gave Isabella strange comfort to know she could be a smashing success as an LA bag lady if the terrorist thing didn't pan out.

It was a plus that she spoke Spanish; it opened a few doors for her. She wished she spoke more languages and had expressed this to the multilingual Viola once.

"My dear," Viola had said. "I was lucky to be born and raised in many cultures and many languages. I understand your Georgia is lovely, but it is hardly the crossroads of the world."

Viola made her blush when she complimented her on her Spanish, a language Viola lacked. Isabella hadn't had much education, but she'd loved Spanish class and watched Spanish television whenever she could. She envied Helena her command of German, but Helena had learned it while stationed in Germany because she was so bored and language lessons were free. Helena also knew some Creole, but had very few occasions to use it.

So, Spanish in Los Angeles was useful. Isabella could be very friendly in both languages, in a spacey, crazy bag lady kind of way. But people in Los Angeles didn't seem to mind much. One of the local shopkeepers even traded her a nice meal in exchange for sweeping his shop and sidewalk. Another shop keeper chased off a teenaged boy who was taunting her. Lucky for that boy; Isabella had become very adept at leading her tormentors into secluded spots and gutting them. This was as much recreation as she was getting in those days.

Once a day, she washed Helena's windshield. It was never the same car, which indicated how bored Helena was if she was stealing a new car every day.

"Where y'at, honey?" Helena asked every day.

"Oh, tolerable, tolerable" Isabella usually replied, but that day she added, "Can you find out about this license plate for me?" She handed a grubby piece of paper into the car under the cover of Helena giving her a dollar. "See you tomorrow," she said, moving off after someone honked at them.

The next day Isabella skipped the windshield and simply slipped into the passenger seat. She put on a pair of dark glasses and tied a scarf around her messy hair. "Let's go take a look at the address," she said.

"You're awfully sure of Miranda, ain'tcha?" Helena teased.

"Shoot, honey, Miranda might screw up, and screw up big, but not very often." She sat back and relaxed for the first time in days. "Where is it?"

"Some crazy place called Boyle Heights," Helena said, handing her the address. "Somewhere down on Cesar Chavez Street."

"They named a whole street–"

"Looks like a big-ass street, too."

"After a...a community organizer?" Isabella asked. "Labor organizer?"

"Yes."

"Lawdy. And I thought the Bob Hope Airport was as crazy as it was gonna git out here."

They rode the rest of the way into Boyle Heights in silence.

The building was a less-than-impressive two story building with storefronts on the ground floor and, supposedly, offices above. They found a place to park with a decent vantage point.

"Well, this is it," Helena said.

"How much cash have you got on you?" Isabella asked.

"Eleven thousand and some change. Want some?"

"Twenty in small bills would be good. Thank you kindly," Isabella said, tucking the cash away. "Let me off at a supermarket so I can get a shopping cart. Can you come back tomorrow?"

"Of course," Helena said, huffily. "Same drill with the windows?"

"That dawg still hunts, don't it?"

"If it ain't broke, don't fix it," Helena said.

"'Yaaa, yu rite, hunee,'" Isabella's imitation got the laugh she was aiming for.

The next day a scraggily looking bag lady waved her to the curb across from the office building to wash her windows.

"How goes it?" Helena asked.

"Some lawyer fella named Kevin Orselli's got a law office in there," Isabella said under the cover of accepting a dollar. "There's a secretary-receptionist gal on the ground floor foyer. I haven't seen anyone else or the car. I think the secretary's a notary; there's a sign in the window. Nice little gal. She gave me a cup of coffee and then chased me off. Bring something to be notarized tomorrow. Meet me behind this building," she said, gesturing to the one Helena was parked in front of.

The secretary was indeed a notary, but there was no sign of Williams that Helena could discern from her brief visit.

"Looks like the office goes all the way to the back of the building and there's a staircase in the back to the second floor," Helena said, driving Isabella away from the Orselli office. "Pretty run-down, but clean; not Williams' usual first-class full-service situation."

"I'm sure I saw him in that car," Isabella said. "I'd bet money on it."

Helena drove to a taco stand several miles away and they had lunch in the car. Isabella asked her to pull around where they could see the alley behind Orselli's building. She asked this mainly so she could finish her large Coke in peace and comfort. They got situated just

138

in time to almost get sideswiped by a large black limousine pulling into the alley.

"That's the car," Isabella said, watching it pull up to one of the storefront back doors. "That's the guy I saw getting out of it at the jail."

"That weaselly-lookin' creep?" Helena asked.

"Yes, ma'am." Isabella was holding her breath. "There! There he is!" she hissed and gasped at the same time. The look on her face was equal parts homicidal and rapturous.

"Are you sure that's Williams? Where's the distinguished graying temples?" Helena asked, squinting at the raven haired man getting out of the limo. "Remember last time we were wrong and damn near killed George Clooney," she added, wishing she had binoculars.

"Yes, I'm sure that's him, even if he's dyeing his hair," Isabella said patiently. "I'm for sure sure it's not George Clooney. What would he be doing down here anyway?"

Helena thought about this for a second, then said, matter-of-factly, "Okay, let's go in and kill him."

They were about to get out their guns when a police car slowly cruised past them. Helena waved and pulled away from the curb. "Maybe we should wait a bit," she suggested, driving around the block.

"Well, drop me here. There's an alley with parking around the back," Isabella said. "You can wait for me over there." She waved at some storefronts.

One of them was a restaurant, very dead at that hour in the afternoon. Helena got a seat at the window with a view of Orselli's office, and in spite of just having eaten, she ordered some chips, guacamole and coffee. She figured the food must be good since there were a pair of cops eating a late lunch. Watching the street, she saw Isabella, looking pathetic, pushing her filthy grocery cart on the opposite side of the street. Several shopkeepers came out with plastic bottles. Then Williams came out of the law office and dropped a plastic bag into Isabella's cart. Isabella must have hit him up for some change, because he dug into his pocket and gave her a dollar. After receiving her thanks, she moved off and he crossed the street. He came into the restaurant, said hello to the cops, and picked up a take-out order. Gracious as ever, he very suavely nodded to Helena on his way out.

After her heart started beating again, Helena finished her coffee, paid her check, left a large tip, and took the chips and guacamole to go. Isabella met her at the car. "Okay, it's him," Helena said, starting the car. "There's too many cops—"

"And lots of guys with guns inside," Isabella said. "I only got a glimpse, but too many to risk it."

They rode in silence for a while.

"Let's come back later and blow him up," Isabella finally suggested. "Is our ammo dump—?"

"Naw, one of the Secure Border idiots led the Marines right to it during the riots," Helena said.

"Ah, damn. Those boys were dumber than a box of rocks."

"But we've got a cache near the Bandini fertilizer plants, not too far from here," Helena smiled at her. "So, we have some, not a lot, but some."

"Well, that's good," Isabella said, bored, watching the warehouses go by. "What about another bazooka attack? Day-yam, that was wild."

"Nope, 'fraid we're all out of bazookas."

While they were stocking up, Kate called to say they were in town, waiting on Ryan's release.

"Yes, yes, we're sure it's him," Helena said patiently into the phone. "He's dyed his hair jet black, but it's definitely him. Isabella panhandled him, that's how close she got." She exchanged smug nods with Isabella. "What? Viola wants to talk to me? Well, put 'er on."

"Uh-oh," Isabella said in an undertone.

"Oh, hi Viola. What? You think we should wait and check with Titania?" Helena asked into the phone.

She frowned at Isabella. "Why? There's standing orders to kill him on sight....Yeah....Yeah....He might know something? Sheeyit, girl, he probably does, but I say we should still kill him...Yes, I'll hold on." She hit the mute button and turned to Isabella. "Sometimes Viola gets all hepped up on protocol or whatever ya call it."

"I think this mission's got her a mite nervous," Isabella said. "She fucked up in Kabul, she fucked up in Baku, she must be worried about fucking up in LA." She smiled dreamily. "Kabul, Baku, those sound like such exotic places."

"I hear they're hellholes," Helena said. "And we've been in Kabul, well, the airport at least."

"I think I need a vacation," Isabella said.

"Really? You blew your chance to be a bag lady for a few weeks," Helena said. "You coulda gone wherever them sand bitches went."

"Helena! Don't call them that!"

"Shee-yit, Isa–" She cut herself off to hit the unmute button. "Yeah, Viola, what did the Boss Lady say? Kill him? Thought so. See ya. Oh, wait, y'all haven't got any bazookas with you? No? Too bad. Good luck with Ryan, he's an obtuse little bastard when you get to know him. Heh!"

"What did she say?" Isabella asked when Helena snapped her phone shut.

"Viola? She said kill Williams," Helena said.

"I mean, what did she say about Ryan?"

"Oh, she said 'You're telling me?' and then she laughed in that irritating way of hers," Helena said.

"He's cute, isn't he?" Isabella asked.

"He's adorable. If you like 'em young and scrawny," Helena said.

They finished packing up the guns, ammo and C4, locked the storage unit and hit the road.

"Ryan, grab your stuff, you're outta here." The sheriff deputy stood by the cell waiting for the shock to wear off Ryan and Bishop.

"What?" Ryan asked stupidly.

"You're sprung and your aunt's here to pick you up," the deputy snapped. "C'mon, I got a whole jail to guard here and you're wasting my time."

Nonplussed, Ryan turned to his protector. "Bishop–"

"Go on, and call Russek when you're out," Bishop said. "You'll let him do that, right, Deputy?"

"Hey, any friend of Russek is someone I'd let use the phone," the deputy said, tapping his foot. "But get a move on. NOW."

Kate, wearing a frumpy floral print, met Ryan as he was coming out at the jail. "Drew, darling!"

"Um, I need to make a phone call." He looked back at the deputy, who'd closed the door and was already walking back into the jailhouse.

"Of course you will," Kate said. "But let's get you something to eat first. You look awfully thin."

"Um..."

"Kate, Aunt Kate," she said, hustling him out of the building and into the hired car. She'd chosen a Lincoln Town Car instead of a limo in order to be more discreet.

"Can I use your phone?" he asked once in the car.

"After lunch, luv," she said, smoothly. "Let's see, I think Taix would be good for lunch. Their food is so lovely, so nutritious, so French."

The driver must have been given this destination in advance because she didn't need to point him towards Echo Park, Taix's home for the past forty-five of its ninety-one year run in Los Angeles.

Ryan looked down at his jeans and t-shirt. "Can I go there like this?" he asked.

"Um, well, no," Kate admitted, surveying his ensemble. After a brief consultation with the driver, they ended up at the Astro Family Restaurant in Silverlake, not far from Russek's place. "I suppose this will do," she thought, ordering a Denver omelet and hoping for the best.

"Can I use your phone?" Ryan asked again.

"I hope this isn't a dodgy omelet," she said, brushing off the question. "Eggs can be such a gamble."

Ryan waited until the waiter poured their coffees. "You know, I don't have an Aunt Kate," he said when they were alone again.

"I know, you must be very trusting to get in a car with someone who doesn't exist." Kate admired her manicure to give him time to say something stupid.

"I dunno, you seem okay," he muttered.

"Just okay?" she asked and he nodded. "Well, anyway, for now I'm your Aunt Kate. I'm also a friend of John Reid, you do remember him, don't you?" She looked on impassively as Drew choked on his coffee. "Yes, I see you do. I'm here to help you." She reached over and pounded him on the back.

"Help me?" Drew gasped when he could. "How?"

"When we are young, we are very trusting," Kate said loftily. "We give our hearts so readily, so easily, to those who cannot love us in return. I want to help you get over John; he was so unkind to you–"

"Not really."

"He abandoned you–"

"Oh, that."

"He was cruel–"

"Hm."

"'Hm'?" Kate asked since her spiel wasn't getting her anywhere. "What do you mean, 'hm'? Didn't John make you love him, then make use of you and then discard you?"

"Oh, I liked him very much, but I've been thinking about it," Drew said with a very serious look on his face. "I don't think I loved him. It was mostly sex and revenge."

"Revenge?"

"Yes, against Reagan and Mademoiselle," he said. "Look, I don't know who you are or how you found me, or what you know about me, but I'm okay with everything that happened. Even though Reagan and Mademoiselle tried to kill me, revenge isn't the answer. I have to let go of the past and get on with my life. I'm in love with someone else now. He's the most important thing to me. That's where my future is, in the future, not in the past."

"That's very wise for one so young," Kate murmured. "How did you gain so much wisdom?"

"I was working with a very good therapist in jail," Drew said, leaning back so the waitress could put down his hamburger platter. "Dr. Smith. She was awesome. I learned a lot about myself in jail," he continued between bites. "I hated jail, but I think I needed to slow down, like, just stop for a while and think things out."

"I see." Kate picked at her overcooked eggs and semi-melted cheese-food. "This man you love, he's a very lucky lad." Drew nodded. "But don't you have some unfinished business with John?"

"No."

"No? Don't you have some computer work for him?" she asked, watching Drew freeze up before her. "I could help you tidy up some loose ends, if you'd like."

"Like...how?" Drew asked.

"Like...I could be a courier for you," she said. "I understand if you don't want to see John–that would be painful–but if you could give me the data you obtained with him, I could get it to him and he would never bother you again. Also, you would have, what's the word? Closure." She saw a familiar face coming heading for their table, but stayed focused on the boy before her.

"Closure...I–" Drew seemed about to dismiss this idea.

"And, of course, some money," she added.

"Oh, money...I–"

"Christ, does the whole fucking LAPD and the Sheriffs have to keep an eye on you, Drew?" Russek asked, looming over their table.

Drew was startled, but joyous as Russek drew him into a hug and a kiss. Kate had noticed Russek when he came in and had foolishly hoped he wouldn't notice them. She smiled blandly across the table at the detective's piercing gaze.

"How dee-do?" she asked, extending her hand across the table. "I am Drew's Aunt Kate."

"That's what the jail told me," Russek said, stealing one of Drew's fries. "They thought it was pretty strange, someone other than me picking up Drew."

"Ah, so you followed us?" she asked politely.

"No, a deputy got the call number off the car you were in and I tracked you down that way," he said, munching more fries. "Strange woman in a strange car; cops notice that kind of thing." He turned to Drew. "I didn't know you had an aunt here."

"These are strange times, Mr. Russek," Kate said before Drew could form a response. "Times for family–known or unknown–to step up. I'm actually Drew's mother's second cousin twice removed. 'Aunt' is simply shorthand for that."

"I see," Russek said thoughtfully. "How did you know my name?"

"Drew told me," she said without a second's hesitation.

Russek looked hard at Drew, who nodded slowly. "I see," Russek said, staring at Drew. "So–"

"You know," Kate cut in, "I really should leave you to your reunion." She slid out of the booth. "I'll be in touch," she added on her way out.

Russek didn't turn his head to watch her go; he stayed focused on his newly liberated lover. "Who was that?" he asked.

"Aunt Kate," Drew said. "I didn't know I had one either."

"Oh. So–" Russek might have continued but the waitress cleared the table and handed them the check. "So, I guess I'm buying your Aunt Kate's lunch," he said, fishing his wallet out.

"Hey, let's go home," Drew asked dreamily. "I mean, can you go home? Do you have to work or something?"

"Nah, the military is doing such a good job policing the streets, the force is letting us take as much time off as we want," Russek said, leading him to his car. "It's very quiet in the city right now."

"Lots of people locked up," Drew said. "That's what they said when I got bounced: they needed the room."

"Yeah," Russek said, pointing the car toward a discreet and affordable motel he knew. He hadn't disabled the listening devices in his place and he didn't want to waste time when he got Drew alone.

"What you mean you need this cell?" Bishop was facing down two deputies trying to throw him out of his nice safe jail. "I just broke it in."

"Out, Bishop. Your lawyer's waiting downstairs," the deputy said, his hand hovering over his nightstick. "Get your shit and get down there."

Bishop's dramatic sigh was not lost on anyone, least of all Kevin Orselli as he led the newly-liberated-on-bail citizen to the waiting limousine.

"Bail? Who paid it? Give it back!" Bishop twisted around in his seat, looking longingly at the jailhouse. "I can get my old cell back!"

"Luke, darling, calm down. A few things have changed." Orselli folded his hands and waited for his cousin to calm down.

"Like fucking what?" Bishop snarled, not so much a question as an accusation.

"Well, we've got a new boss–"

"What happened to Emil?"

"Car accident in a parking garage. So the new guy is really sharp, really ruthless, too. We've been making money–"

"Legit?"

"And otherwise, too, yes, hand over fist–"

"Fist. Using your fist these days, Kevin?"

"Yes, and everything else. So–"

"Hey, this ain't the way to Boyle Heights." Bishop glared out the tinted window. "Where the fuck–"

"I was gonna tell you," Orselli interrupted. "The office blew up."

"Really?" Bishop asked, with an inquisitive sneer. "How?"

"I was blowing Mr. Lopez in the car–"

"Who?"

"The new boss, Lazarus Lopez."

"Go on."

"Where was I?"

"Blowing Lopez."

"Oh, yes, and he hadn't come when we got to the office, so we stayed in the car," Orselli said, primly. "The driver went into the office and then the doors and windows blew out."

"Before or after Lopez came?"

"Simultaneously."

Bishop stared out at a city he hated, fought, and bore the battle scars from. He'd have to go back into it and kill or be killed. He was starting to look forward to it. He was also starting to feel sexy again after his long bout of jailhouse self-control with his pretty cellmate. "He blew. The office blew," he murmured, reaching for Orselli and shoving him to the floor. "Show me."

Drew drowsed peacefully in Russek's arms on motel sheets, staring at the nicotine-stained cottage cheese ceiling. Russek had helped him shower off the smell of the jailhouse and kissed him long and hard as he jerked them both off in the shower. Drew had missed kissing the most, and he missed kissing Russek most of all. Once in the unfamiliar bed, they'd spent a lot of time learning each other again.

"You've lost weight," Russek said, running his hands over Drew's jutting hipbones.

"The food really sucked." Drew curled closer into

Russek's barrel chest.

"Bishop took good care of you, huh?"

"Yeah." His answer satisfied Russek, so Drew didn't elaborate on how Bishop was taking care of him in the mornings.

"What about this Samsa character?" Russek asked, leaning back to look at him.

"Oh, him, I kind of forgot about him," Drew said. "He helped Bishop keep 'em off me. He was kind of nice. Had a crazy name, though."

"How so?"

"He said his name was Gregor Samsa," Drew said, sleepily. "But Gregor Samsa was the guy in the Kafka story who turned into a giant cockroach."

Drew barely heard Russek's thoughtful "Huh," as he dozed off. Samsa was a mysterious guy like John Reid. Like Mademoiselle and Aunt Kate. Lots of mysterious people in his life, too many. Remembering was fine, but dreaming was better. He hoped he wouldn't be dreaming of John Reid, giant cockroaches, flowery perfumes, twisty streets, apple tea, and listening drowsily to the morning prayer call at the little hotel near the Blue Mosque. He only wanted to dream about Paul Russek now and always.

Chapter 11

Emotional Bankruptcy

The Department Manager sat back in his chair and seemed to be admiring her. At least that was all Titania could surmise from his thoughtful silence while her more immediate supervisor seethed and fidgeted next to her. She was used to briefing men who slowly began to respect her intelligence and then, after deciding she was at least useful, let their guard down. That was when Titania usually moved in for the kill, if only to see the look of dumbfounded shock on their smug faces. There was no finer rush for her than taking out an adversary, especially one that liked her. It wasn't always necessary to kill them; sometimes just driving them to suicide was enough. But the dead are dead and usually don't have many surprises left in them. She wasn't wondering if she'd have to kill these men, but when and how best to do it.

However, at that moment, she was not just narrating Viola's nearly-genius urban terror tactics, but reveling in them. But all good things must come to an end, and after she finished her analysis of the post-riot events in Los Angeles, she merely folded her hands and waited for the next question. It was not what she expected.

The Department Manager roused himself and asked her if she'd like more coffee. Then he sent the Section Manager out for three fresh coffees, café lattes this time. "So," he asked when the Section Manager's footsteps faded away. "Why do you hate Warren Williams so much?"

"Have you met him?" she asked.

"No, he's not likely to stop by a lowly bureaucrat's

office any time soon."

"Oh, he might," she said, breezily. "Just to give you a glimpse of his impossible glamour. He'd be friendly, too, the kind of man you could drink single-malt scotch and smoke cigars with. And afterwards he'd know your innermost secrets and you'd be hard pressed to remember the color of his eyes or a word of anything he said."

"He's a phantom, they tell me."

"He's Death." Titania surprised herself as she hissed these words with murderous vehemence, giving the Department Manager a glimpse of her passion before whisking her professional veil over it again.

"How so?"

The Department Manager's cool question almost surprised her. She had to remind herself that she was dealing with a man just as much of a professional as she was. But with the one enormous advantage of being a man in a man's world.

"I've never seen him in a battlefield situation," she said, carefully choosing her words. "I'm told he's a gallant soldier, no matter which side he's on. It's his personal life where he lulls his victims, or lovers as some would call them, into a stupor and leaves them to their fate, which is usually death or something worse. I suppose the reason this Ryan child survived at all was because Russek protected him, in jail and out of it. If Ryan had died in the Los Angeles County lock-up, Williams would have made a tragic show of mourning his true love and written the whole mess off as an amusing loss. He's like that; striking sentimental poses while planning his next move."

"Are these conclusions drawn from, ah, personal experience?"

"Oh, heaven's no, sir, I wouldn't get within ten feet of the man," Titania said, mentally waving a fan and batting her eyelashes while her face remained its usual professional mask, possibly more so. "No, this is pure observation and research. Williams has weaknesses; the biggest being that he believes he believes in love. It's a luxury he can ill afford, and yet he stubbornly clings to this idea of himself as a warm, loving, wonderful human being." She paused to read the Department Manager's face and found it a cipher. "And yet, Williams has killed more people in the name of 'love' or 'patriotism' or 'justice' and believes he is a hero as he washes the blood of the good and the bad and everything in between off his hands."

"This is the world we live in, Agent," the Department Manager said blandly.

"And made by men like Williams, to reward men like Williams, to spawn more men like Williams," Titania said. "My group and our work are in reaction to Williams and Williamsism. That's why we hate him so much and try to kill him as often as we can."

"I'm surprised, with as much talent as you have in your group, you haven't succeeded yet." He tilted his head at the approaching footsteps.

"He's lucky, too," Titania said, listening to the same thing. "And luck, I've concluded, is the most important blessing you can have in this brutal world." She fixed a bland smile on her mouth and rose to help her Section Manager pass out the large lattes.

Warren Williams did not believe in luck. He believed in destiny. His destiny, mainly.

Sometimes he wondered if anyone other than himself even existed. But these were isolated thoughts that adrenaline, intrigue, or sex easily dispelled. Oh, and love, there was always love, and at that moment in Los Angeles, under an assumed name and a head of dyed-black hair, Williams was still deeply in love with Drew Ryan. Williams knew this because he wasn't in love with anyone else at that moment, so he must still be in love with Ryan.

But he was even more enamored of the information Ryan grabbed at the DARPA front before all hell broke loose. Information Williams' reliable sources, good old boys, thugs, and various interested persons had yet to unearth. There was one person alive who knew where that data was, and, in addition to being at liberty again, he was adorable.

Life was so uncertain for Williams; he knew there could be a bullet around the next corner, a bomb under his bed, or even something as mundane as a car accident to take him out. So he lived with as much zest as caution. His experience with men was limited to topping, receiving blowjobs from beautiful men, and, on very rare occasions and under extraordinary circumstances, giving head. He had to be swept up in the moment to do so, which was seldom, since Williams was always on guard and having his face buried in another man's crotch distracted him very much.

And yet Williams was utterly fascinated by every inch of Drew's body. He'd taken his time deflowering the young man, spent hours caressing him to new and higher climaxes before gently opening and entering him. While waiting for Drew's passport in Ankara, there had been time for love. In a comfortable safe house with plenty of privacy in which to explore each other, Williams had grown fond of the young man. Even Drew's endless rambling about his limited experience in life, the internet, things that annoyed or delighted him were worth sifting through to learn what the lad knew about La Directrice's operation in Electricland. Williams had simply laid back and let Drew's stream of consciousness wash over him. He learned that La Directrice was more vulnerable than he'd ever imagined. A frontal assault was impossible, but there was a way to her through cyberspace or whatever it was called (like Eskimos are said to have many names for snow, Drew had many names for the internet, which was the most important thing to him) that might be more financial than martial. She was elusive, and her people—Mademoiselle, the Cracker, the Lotus—were lethal. His one experience with the Lotus had nearly killed him and even after he'd escaped and she'd been captured, La Directrice had mounted an assault on the Bagram torture center that left dozens dead. All to rescue one damaged woman. This seemed a waste of time and resources to Williams, but even La Directrice's sentimental attachment to her people made her stronger, rather than weaker. This annoyed him more than he could express. La Directrice and her operation, especially this level of loyalty and nobility among women, obsessed and fascinated him beyond all reason. Would anyone have risked so much to rescue him? He didn't think so.

Los Angeles, for Williams, had been a torture of waiting for Drew to get out of jail. The weather was lovely, but Williams, grim and determined, could not enjoy it. He could not enjoy Orselli's spectacular blowjob technique, something Drew never mastered or even got good at. Nor was Williams able to enjoy the best of every kind of cuisine on the planet available in Los Angeles. Traffic was horrible, but he could have eaten his way around the city and simply enjoyed the time he spent in traffic digesting it.

No, he had one focus: getting the data Drew stole in the DARPA front. It was obvious to Williams that it was La Directrice's financial information, the funding streams she used to keep her organization going. The real funds, not the chump change she got from the government, but the accounts into which were pumped the lifeblood of her operations that were sucked out of the hooks she had in God knew whom. Looking over Drew's shoulder, Williams had paled at some of the names or anagrams of names of the "donors." Some of them were supposed to be dead, which made them very exotic angels for La Directrice. Some of them were funding both sides of the "good" fight, keeping the world off-balance while they and their respectable and illicit businesses looted the honest earnings of the world's workers.

Williams had very little ideology beyond his own high opinion of himself, but he knew La Directrice had even less. She wasn't such a mystery to him, she was a woman quietly building an empire on the bones of her enemies. Williams could almost respect her for that if she wasn't so intent on killing him. Her crew were more of a mystery: he had no idea how many people really worked for La Directrice beyond the two women he'd met. He thought there was an American woman from Alabama or thereabouts, but there could have been ten of them as well as one. Based on the ease with which La Directrice moved her operations around Central Asia and Asia Minor, Williams concluded that she had operatives or cells scattered about the area, but again, until he got the funding information, and could blackmail an answer out of her, he had no real way of knowing. The internet operations were impressive, but Williams could barely check his email, so he assumed La Directrice had an IT department the size of Microsoft. Perhaps it was Microsoft: anything was possible with that brilliant, ruthless woman.

His goal was not to destroy her, or master her, or even tame her, but to understand her. La Directrice mesmerized and terrified Williams in equal measure. She was like a deadly, beautiful spider sitting in her web waiting for the world to prostrate itself under her chelicerae so she could sink in her fangs and drink deep. While Williams and his ilk thrashed around the globe, La Directrice merely raised an elegantly manicured hand and sent one of her crones to wreck havoc. Williams could only follow in awe, horror, and an ever stronger determination to defang his goddess and her priestesses.

One night in bed, after sweet and clumsy sex, Williams had tried to explain all this to Drew. Drew said he thought Williams was obsessed; no one was that powerful. But Williams had reminded Drew of Mademoiselle's seduction and abandonment and Drew, in his very limited experience of women, began to understand. Women were meant to nurture and support men. When they did anything else, they became mistresses of their fates and crueler mistresses of all they surveyed.

Ah, Drew...Williams ached with longing for his young lover, although he was having a little trouble remembering much about him. Perhaps this Bishop person could refresh his memory somewhat.

And so Williams was completely horrified that the bristly-headed motherfucker in filthy, dried-blood-stained jeans and wife-beater, standing before him in steel-tipped motorcycle boots, had been anywhere near his precious Drewling, let alone possibly touching that adorable young man.

"Did you have your filthy paws on Drew?" Williams snarled, remembering to give his voice Lopez's accent.

Bishop heaved a deep sigh before springing for the swarthy sharpie motherfucker's throat. He was dropped to the floor with a well-aimed blow just below his Adam's apple that made him see stars and black out. He came to to the sound of Orselli insisting that "He cleans up real pretty," and looking up into the coldest blue eyes he'd ever seen. Furthermore, Bishop noticed that whatever this cat's name was, he was a white guy with dyed black hair. But whatever this Lopez guy was, he'd dropped Bishop's bad ass with one blow and earned some serious mano-a-mano respect. Talk about making a killer first impression.

After a little more staring, Lopez moved back enough for Orselli to help Bishop to his feet. Bishop narrowed his eyes and tried to look tough, but not so tough that Lopez, regarding him from under hooded eyes, might feel he needed to kill him.

"You know where Drew Ryan is. Bring him to me," Lopez said, coldly. "If I see you again without him, I'll kill you."

Bishop was still thinking up a snappy come-back as Orselli hustled him out of the room.

"Are you nuts?" Orselli demanded once they were in the car. "That's the new boss."

"Eh, maybe I got the jailhouse jitters," Bishop said dismissively. He didn't want to discuss his impression that the new boss was way too grand for his cousin's little con-man operations. Why would a guy like Lopez want in on that? And the first thing he asks Bishop for is little Drew Ryan? Bishop was paranoid, but this guy was making him super paranoid. "Where the fuck we going?"

"To the spa to steam the eau de jail out of you and then to get some new clothes. Here's a phone to keep in touch with."

"I like these clothes," Bishop said, admitting to himself that what he was wearing would scare Drew, which he'd like to avoid doing. He pocketed the cell phone without even looking at it. He hated phones, computers, ATMs, and all kind of impersonal technoshit like that. Bishop was a hands-on kind of guy.

"We'll get some just like them," Orselli said. "Just cleaner. You can keep the moto-psycho boots."

"Don't make fun of my boots, cousin," Bishop growled over Orselli humming "These boots are made for ass-kickin'."

After celebrating his release from jail Drew settled back into life with Russek as best he could. He had trouble sleeping and his appetite was off. He was easily startled and was edgier than usual. Russek assured him it was just the post-jailhouse jumps and to let it run its course. He offered to take Drew to a doctor who specialized in post-traumatic stress disorders, but Drew was doctor-averse and declined. He said he'd rather just ride it out.

Getting back into sex with Russek had been tricky. Once Drew put his foot down and demanded that they stop having sex in anonymous motels in obscure parts of Los Angeles, he and Russek started to get to know each other again. Even Drew had to admit his jailhouse sexual escapades, such as they were, had changed him a little. He tried not to show any impatience with Russek's sensitivity and trying to read him. That might be fine someday, but just then Drew wanted to be held down and fucked really hard. This desire shocked him somewhat. His first lover, John, had been smooth and elegant, and Drew merely had to follow his lead in everything. Russek was gentle, wry, and considerate in bed and about the same out of bed. But Bishop and Samsa, restrained as they were, had shocked and unsettled Drew. They never asked for what they wanted, they just took it. Yes, they were nice about it, but lurking beneath their brusque and unrefusable actions, were brutal men who would have hurt him badly if he'd refused. Now, in retrospect, Drew's stressed-out mind reformulated his lack of consent into permission or even willing surrender. Strong desire to see these men again warred with terror that he would see them again and would be unable to resist them. "Dear God," he thought. "What if they showed up at the same time? And what if Paul wasn't here to protect me?" He had nightmares; sometimes they woke Russek, sometimes not. He told Russek they were about the jail. Russek didn't press him.

Housework became a solace and a break from the internet for Drew. He'd gotten as far as the login for Electricland before he backed away from it. It was a dangerous, deadly place for him, he knew that now, and he knew he was no match for it. "So what do I do?" he asked himself repeatedly. "Spend the rest of my life living with Paul and writing WordPress widgets?" He shuddered at the thought and got back to work dissolving layers of grime from Russek's kitchen counters with Pink Grapefruit-scented Method All Surface spray cleaner.

He was wiping down the stove when Samsa knocked on the door and came in. "Ya know that's dangerous," he said in his laconic drawl. "Ya should lock yer doors, ya never know who's gonna come in."

"Samsa!" Even Drew thought he was way too happy to see this particular man. "You're out! When–?"

"A few days after ya," Samsa said, moving around

the room, as if deciding to light somewhere. "They let the not-very-violent ones out a few days after they sprung ya."

"I, um, thought you were pretty violent," Drew stammered. "In a good way, y'know?"

"Well, I wasn't in for violent crime," Samsa said, moving close. "They got me on traffic warrants."

Drew was hypnotized and could only nod when Samsa told him they were going out. And yet Drew didn't obey immediately. He was halfway into Samsa's arms when Samsa pulled back.

"Ya expecting someone?" he asked, taking a surreptitious peek out the window.

"No." Only then Drew heard the car door slam; he'd completely missed it pulling into the driveway. He looked around Samsa's shoulder. "Oh, it's Paul."

"Russek?"

"Yeah."

Samsa slid a cell phone into Drew's hand. "I'll call ya on this," he whispered, looking over his shoulder. "Ya can call me, too."

Drew barely had time to put the phone in his pocket and step back before Russek pushed open his front door, glanced at his boyfriend, and then gave the rough looking stranger a hard-ass cop-look. "Hi," he grated out.

Samsa said, "Hi," returning Russek's look with his own badass traffic-violator look.

"Friend of yours, Drew?" Russek asked, never breaking eye-contact with Samsa.

"He's the guy from the jail," Drew said, snapping out of his daze and remembering his manners. "Samsa, this is Paul Russek. Paul this is Gregor Samsa."

The men did not shake hands or even nod.

Samsa cracked first.   "Yeah, Drew, see ya...maybe."

"Oh, okay."

Russek just said, "Uh-huh," and escorted Samsa out the door. "What was he doing here?" he asked Drew the second the door was closed and bolted.

"He came to see me," Drew said innocently.

"Uh-huh."

"What are you doing home?" Drew asked when Russek didn't go on.

"I was in the area," he said. "Let's get some lunch."

They went to Astro's where Russek didn't mention Samsa or that the precinct surveillance team had called him when Drew's visitor started talking on the listening devices. Russek had removed the bugs only from his bedroom. A man needs a certain amount of privacy, even when it's in the interest of the greater good to keep tabs on his lover.

"And who the hell is Gregor Samsa?" Titania asked when Miranda replayed the audio from Russek's love nest to her.

"He was a character in a Kafka novel," Viola said on the speaker phone.

"Oh, yes, the bloke who turns into a cockroach," Kate added.

"Damn, I've got to read this book," Helena muttered just loud enough to be heard.

"I see," Titania said before Isabella, if she was there, could jump in with an observation. "We're dealing with an agent. But whose?"

"Just what we all needed," Isabella said. "Another joker in the pack."

"Who could get an agent in and out of the jail that easily?" Miranda asked, or rather suggested. "Let's start looking at those people."

"I reckon that leaves out the Vatican and the Mormons," Helena said dryly.

"Probably," Titania said over the laugh this got. "You asked for tranquillizer jabs and night goggles. I've FedExed the jabs to your hotel. I'm sending the night goggles UPS ground. I hope you have an explanation if you're asked."

"We'd say we need them for spying on our husbands," Kate said, sounding so reasonable anyone would buy it. "Dangerous, though, FedExing the jabs."

"They're disguised as lipsticks," Titania said. "Don't stick yourselves accidentally. Or on purpose," she added just before cutting off the connection.

Chapter 12

A Gun as Lovely as a Tree

"You do realize, Agent Titania, that Cardinal Mahoney and the Huntington Foundation are still furious over the events you orchestrated," her Section Manager was snarling at her.

Titania had been contemplating the Department Manager, with whom she felt a budding, though silent, rapport. She snapped out of it to give the little weasel she reported to more directly her full attention. "I can't imagine why," she said, sounding bored. "All we did was give some very deserving nuns a day in the park, high tea, and, yes, we did rip up a little turf, but the Huntington has armies of gardeners to fix up such things." She paused to let her boss fume and the Department Manager chuckle. "After all, the Church is evicting their nuns left and right to sell their convents to pay for the molestation lawsuits. Do you ever hear of priests or monks losing their homes and having to scramble for, well, anything? It seemed like a very small and sisterly gesture to use the nuns as cover. And by all reports, they enjoyed themselves mightily."

"You...you..." her Section Manager could only sputter as his boss simply cracked up.

"Really," Titania said serenely. "It was the least we could do."

The call had come, not on Samsa's cell phone or Russek's phone or even Drew's own phone, but over Skype. Since the whole mess in Baku, Drew wasn't getting many Skype calls; all his old internet buddies were steering clear of him. So he answered right away and was shocked to hear it was his "Aunt Isabella" inviting him to meet her at the Huntington Gardens in Pasadena in a few hours. She claimed to have the information he never got from his "Aunt Kate."

"I–"

"You do still want to know what really happened in Baku and then in Los Angeles, don't you, Drew?" the silky voice asked him.

"Los An–?"

"They're connected, you know that," she said smoothly. "Or you suspect that. Don't you want to know which one—Reid or Mademoiselle or both—made a fool of you? Or have you let go of it, come to terms with it, are you at peace with it? Have you tied up all the loose ends that might come back to bite you in the ass?"

She was quiet while he thought about this. Finally he admitted that he wanted to know and there were a few loose ends that were bothering him. He agreed to meet her and pulled up the website and directions to confirm the directions she was giving him, which were impeccable.

"How will I know you?" he asked.

"I'm a Benedictine nun," she said. "You'll know me by my habit."

Drew took Russek's car. Russek had an unmarked police car he used when he was on duty, so he left his personal car for Drew. Drew hadn't driven it much; he wasn't leaving the house much, mainly to get groceries and take-out food. Except for the twisty Pasadena freeway part, he didn't find the drive to Pasadena especially arduous or the Huntington difficult to find. The grounds of the former estate took up several square blocks just east of CalTech, which was something Drew now also wanted to explore, but it would have to wait until he'd met up with "Aunt Sister Isabella."

But once he got to the Huntington, parked and picked up the ticket she had waiting for him, finding her became tricky because the gardens were full of all kinds of nuns. Not that Drew could tell the difference between the Orders, but there seemed to be all kinds of women in long robes and wimples, or modest dresses with their hair covered. There were a few in modest pantsuits who also seemed to be nuns or were with more traditionally dressed nuns. It seemed to Drew that there were few or no civilians in the park that afternoon. Well, it was the middle of the week, most people worked, so it was possible there weren't any regular people there.

He strolled aimlessly though the well kept grounds, nodding to nuns who smiled pleasantly at him. He could only hope his aunt would find him. It was late Spring and the gardens were especially beautiful in the soft air and gentle sunshine. Drew hardly noticed them except when he had to skirt the carp ponds or the bonsai displays. He did pause in the Zen garden to muse on the raked gravel. Raked gravel was supposed to be important, but the significance was lost on Drew.

However, it was in the Zen garden that Sister Isabella picked him up. "Soothing, isn't it, Drew?" she asked, suddenly standing next to him in a huge black habit right out of the "Sound of Music."

He jumped, but recovered. "Um...Aunt Isabella?"

"Of course," she said. "Walk with me, Drew." She gestured for him to follow her. "Can you tell the difference between the nuns here today?" she asked, conversationally.

Drew shook his head.

"It's hard to tell because in their humility and devotion to religious life, they're not supposed to stand out," she said serenely. "Those wearing small veils pinned to their hair, dowdy dark skirts, sweaters, and very big crucifixes could be any order: Ursulines, Nazareth Sisters, Salesians, Sisters of this, Sisters of that, et cetera. But those nuns in the long brown robes with the coarse belt are Franciscans. The ones all in white with the black veils are Dominicans. There are dozens of convents, communities, schools where nuns teach in Los Angeles. The only nuns you won't see here today are the cloistered sisters, the women who've walled themselves up alive to get away from this sick world." She sighed heavily and nodded to a passing group of nuns, who nodded back, but gave her a strange look.

They strolled silently away from the camellias and koi ponds until they were in the sparsely populated sub-tropical garden where they were out of sight of the galleries and unlikely to be overheard.

"Thank you kindly for meeting me here," she said softly.

"You said you could help me," Drew said. "I need to know what really happened in Baku."

"You became the pawn of a very evil man," she said, almost sadly. "A man who stripped you of your innocence, used you, and abandoned you." She glanced at him. "A man who will not leave you in peace until he gets what he thinks you got before you were captured by the LAPD," she added when he didn't go on.

"How do you know about that?" Drew asked.

"There are rumors," she said. "There are always rumors. There was a rumor that that man was killed in an explosion, but his body was not identified among the dead. He cheats death, he cheated you, and he will hound you into your grave unless you allow me to help you."

"How?"

"You downloaded some information from a server the night you were arrested," she said, gazing gently at him. "Give it to me and I'll free you of John Reid."

Drew, nonplussed hearing the words "downloaded" and "server" coming from the yards of black fabric standing next to him, started at the sound of Reid's name. He was trying to forget everything about him and concentrate on Paul (and, unwillingly, Bishop and Samsa). "I don't know what you're talking about," he said in a squeaky voice.

"You lie."

This shocked him, considering what the source was

wearing. He cleared his throat. "I don't have what you're talking about," he said more firmly.

"You still lie."

"I really don't have it."

"You can get it."

"No, I can't."

"You lie."

Drew stepped in front of her. "Stop calling me a liar!" Several passing nuns glanced at them.

"Bless your little heart. I'll stop calling you a liar," she said, matching his furious stare with a calm one. "When you stop being one."

"Drew!" Russek was crossing the lawn.

"Paul?" Drew's voice was squeaky again, but he was looking past Russek at a man he just barely got a glimpse of before he slipped behind some shrubbery.

By then Russek had joined them and he nodded to the nun. "Oh, Paul, this is my Aunt Isabella," Drew stammered.

"You seem to have a lot of aunts all of a sudden," Russek said, staring hard at Isabella.

"We're all just a large and lovely family. Excuse me," Isabella said, catching sight of the man Drew had been staring at.

"Now hold on, Sister." Russek put his hand on her arm to detain her. She stiff-armed him onto his ass and took off into the flocks of nuns heading for their complimentary high tea.

Russek lost her in the sea of religious women, but he did find her veil and parts of her habit. "Your Sister Auntie is some kind of stripteaser nun, I guess," he observed wryly to Drew right before they were nearly run over by two women on a motorcycle.

Complete pandemonium reigned as the bike roared across the grass and through flowerbeds chasing something or someone. By that time there were guards running and nuns scattered everywhere.

But Russek and Drew were surrounded by their own magic circle of tranquility. Russek was wondering who these crazy women stalking Drew were and Drew was wondering why Samsa was at the Huntington with them. Was he with Sister Aunt Isabella or did he follow Drew there? And why would he? And while he was thinking about this, what the fuck was Paul doing there?

"Paul?"

"Yeah?"

"Why are you here?"

"I have LoJack on my car," he said, smiling at his adorable lover. "I followed you."

"You followed me?" Drew was aghast.

"Yeah, I followed you," Russek repeated. "I'm worried about you. There're crazy women after you. Who the hell was that at Astro's and just now?"

"Um...I don't know," Drew said, sifting through the truth for just the right amount of it. "They wanted to talk to me about John Reid."

"Why?"

"They seem to know him," Drew said. "Better than I do."

Russek thought about this for a moment. "That's not good, Drew," he said. Drew merely shrugged, so Russek took him to tea at the restaurant. The police came halfway through it, but didn't ask them any questions.

Meanwhile, Helena and Isabella stole a tour bus each and agreed to meet at the Hamburger Hamlet a few hours later. Isabella got there first and was waiting for the bartender to notice her and take her to-go order. She was still waiting when Helena arrived.

"Getting ignored?" she asked the fuming woman.

"How much do you want a hamburger?" Isabella asked.

"I could go for Chinese."

The bartender asked if he could take their order. Isabella drew her gun and pointed it at his left eye.

"Oh, my God, lady, I have kids," he hissed in terror.

"They'll get over it," she said pulling the trigger.

The bar area was fairly deserted, so they only had to kill a few witnesses on their way out. Helena had stolen a nondescript Honda Civic, which they abandoned at a Metro station to take public transportation to Chinatown.

Back at the hotel, Viola and Kate were packing to move to the Biltmore downtown. They were sick of the Westside and decided to be closer to Russek and Drew's love nest. But not too close.

"Merde," was all Viola could say after Isabella ran down that afternoon's events.

"How did bloody Russek get there?" Kate asked. "And who was the mysterious man Drew was looking at? And how did he get there?"

"Damn if we know," Helena said, irritated that they had more questions than answers than ever before. "We were just in the middle of the mess back there."

"This thing is going pear-shaped," Kate agreed. "Should we call Titania?" she asked the brooding Viola.

"No," Viola said. Her voice was cold, but her face was unreadable. "Being nice isn't getting results. We're also running out of time; one can only terrorize a city for so long. We must get that boy somewhere quiet and make him talk."

The other three women nodded in agreement. They ordered tea and continued packing for the next day's move.

Russek was starting to ask a lot of difficult questions Drew didn't have easy answers for. He didn't know who his aunts were, he didn't know who Samsa was, and he didn't know why all these crazy things were happening to him. Rather pointedly, Russek pointed out that these crazy things were happening to them, not just Drew.

"Yes...yes," Drew said, stepping into Paul's safe, loving arms. Drew was doing his best not to pretend Paul was Reid, Bishop, or Samsa in their intimate moments. He deeply hoped Paul didn't notice, but, as far as Drew could tell, Paul was enjoying himself too much to notice anything other than their mutual pleasure. He did his best to damp down his curiosity about sex with other men, or anything else about other gay men. Paul was the only admittedly gay man he knew; he knew in Reid's case and assumed in Samsa's and Bishop's case they were merely making an exception for him. This was oddly flattering to Drew, but he also realized he was some kind of whim or stopgap to them. Or something. It was all too much for him to think about most of the time.

Drew was trying to stay off the internet as much as possible. This was very difficult, like some kind of withdrawal, but housework helped clear his mind as it exercised his body. Intellectually, he knew it was paranoid to think Electricland was stalking him on the web. But as crazy as it was, Drew was aware that the siren song of Electricland might be too strong for him to resist. It was possible he could be drawn in again, pulled under, and drowned. So he spent his days deep cleaning the musty dusty corners of Paul's little house. All this housework was also very necessary; Paul's housekeeper had simply stopped coming to clean the house after the one time Drew saw her, and Paul wasn't very tidy.

Drew was making real progress in the bedroom and was planning to dust the living room, especially the mantle and bookcases, when he got a bad case of cabin fever. Knowing the car was LoJacked he knew he couldn't go anywhere exciting (even if he knew where that was), so the grocery store a few miles away was his destination. He didn't notice the car following him, nor did he notice the man in the car watching him struggle with a huge decision in the grocery store parking lot: whether to go grocery shopping or go to the gay biker bar across the street. He locked the car and crossed the street to the Gallodrome Bar and Grill.

Watching from his car, Bishop could only groan, "Oh God, Drew, don't do this to me," as he watched the little idiot vanish into a biker bar that was rough even by Bishop's broad standards. But he was on a mission, as much for himself as for Lopez; he was going to go into the Gallodrome and get Drew.

Inside at the bar, a biker was already hitting on sweet little Drew, but he backed off fast when Drew's face lit up at the sight of Bishop.

"Bishop!"

"Hey, hiya, kid," he growled, giving the biker a 'scram motherfucker' look that would have scared Charlie Manson off. "What the hell you doing in here?" he asked after the bartender brought him a beer.

"I...I came here to think," Drew said, lamely.

"Oh, man, you gotta be kidding me. Nobody comes in a place like this to think. They come here to get laid," Bishop laughed. "Or killed," he added, grimly.

Drew was silent as he drank his beer, while Bishop, also silent, drank his beer. "So, you're out, too," he finally said.

"Yeah, I'm out," Bishop said staring at the cash register without seeing it. "I'm out and the city is even worse than when I went in. But here I am: out in the shit again."

"I'm sorry," Drew said. Russek had explained that Bishop was happier in jail than out, but unlucky with being able to stay inside. "Couldn't you do something minor, a, what's it called? A misdemeanor to get put back in?"

"Nah, too dangerous right now, they shooting shoplifters on sight these days," Bishop told him. "The jails are jammed to the max now, and my fucking attorney would get me out right way."

"He must be a good attorney," Drew said.

"He sucks as an attorney," Bishop said, trying not to think of blowjobs. "But he useful sometimes." He turned his head and found Drew looking at him very intensely and trembling. The huge dewy eyes were irresistible but his trembling nearly sent Bishop over the edge. With massive effort he controlled himself. "You cold, Drew?" he asked.

"Bishop...let's go to a motel."

"I can't go to a motel with you!" Heads turned to stare at them, Bishop stared them down.

"Why not?" Drew hissed the question.

"Something might happen in a motel," Bishop said, more quietly. "We might have sex or something."

"That's why I want to go to one." Drew laid a tentative hand on Bishop's nearest massive forearm. "Or we can go back to Paul's place, I–"

Bishop's horrified gasp cut him off. "You crazy? We can't go to Russek's place," he said. "He'd kill us both."

"He wouldn't know."

"Oh, he'd know," Bishop said. "I'd tell him."

"Why?" Drew looked hurt.

"I'm suicidal." Bishop ran his hand over his head stubble. "Look, I'm supposed to bring you to meet this guy, Lopez. You know him?"

"No, I don't know anyone named Lopez," Drew said, puzzled. "What does he want?"

"He wants you," Bishop said blandly. "More than that, I dunno." Some silence went by. "Hey, listen, I'm not going to a motel with you because I don't fuck nice boys living with cops. It's a policy I have."

"And you don't want to," Drew said bitterly.

"I didn't say that, kid," Bishop said. He met Drew's humid gaze with his own polar one and was giving some serious thought to revising his sex policy— never fuck anyone you like—or at least making Drew the exception that proved the rule, or something, when a fight broke out in the pool table area. "Let's go," he said, guiding Drew safely to the door. "Before this place corrupts us."

Outside, Bishop walked Drew to his car and got the kid's cell phone number.

"How can I reach you?" Drew asked.

"Just think about me," Bishop said.

As they parted, neither of them noticed the woman

watching them from her car across the street.

"Oh, Christ, that's Helena," Titania said, looking at the screen over Miranda's shoulder.

"It's very blurry and dark, Titania," Mirada said reasonably. "I PhotoShopped it to see it better. Here's what they have." She clicked her mouse a few times.

"And the police don't have PhotoShop?" Titania asked. "Don't be silly, Miranda, they're doing the same thing you did."

"But it's still a mess," Miranda said. "I had a hard time recognizing her."

"That would be partly due to your Asperger's Syndrome." Recovering her poise somewhat, Titania asked, "Where did this come from?"

"It was found on a body at a Hamburger Hamlet massacre in Pasadena," Miranda said.

"Aaah, Pasadena, I've read it's a lovely town," Titania said, buying herself some time to think. "Roughly how far from the Huntington?" Miranda told her. "Ah. And could you scan the news for other strange, probably lethal, events that day, particularly that afternoon in Pasadena?" A few moments later, Miranda rattled off several car thefts, murders, and vehicle collisions, including two with driverless tour buses. "Ah. Could you get Viola on a secure line? Thank you, dear. I'd like to know who was having a bad day after the Huntington action went phut."

If Titania was expecting outrage from Viola, she didn't get it. All she got was Viola's usual admiration for the two American women's ability to improvise on the fly and end up in a good restaurant afterwards. She scoffed at the cell phone photo, saying it showed nothing incriminating and was too blurry for anyone to really see who it was. Viola then segued onto another, more pressing subject, and asked if Titania and Miranda had identified Ryan's mysterious boyfriend/visitor yet. The one who might have been at the Huntington with Helena and Isabella.

"No," Titania said. "Miranda's scouring transmission history that uses similar naming architecture, but nothing so far. That would at least tell us what group we're dealing with. There can't be that many that could get a man in and out of that jail like that."

"How many enemies has America now?" Viola asked.

"Many, very many," Titania said. "But this isn't about America, it's about us, someone is on to us, and I need to know who."

"I see. That would narrow the field to several dozen possible organizations," Viola said dryly. "Has Miranda gotten the cell phone photo from Isabella yet?"

"Yes, who is it?" Titania asked.

"That's what we want to know. He followed Ryan into a gay bar and then they parted. I'm not an expert on gay men, but isn't that unusual? Don't they usually go somewhere together?"

"Only in the stereotype."

"Pardon?"

"Yes, that is odd, isn't it? What did Isabella do then?" Titania asked hurriedly.

"She followed 'Boyfriend 2' until he lost her," Viola said. She waited until Titania finished sighing. "Don't blame her for not being good at following cars in this traffic. We're saboteurs, not detectives."

"Viola–"

"And we're running out of time," Viola cut her off. "We need to act. No one has the data he stole, they would have done something with it by now, we would know. You and Miranda have covered those tracks and all the tracks around it, we don't need to know exactly what it was."

"Yes."

"So we can kill him," Viola said. "And Russek, too, since he's the only other person who might know or figure out where the data is." She paused. "And at this point knowing Ryan is dead would make me very happy."

"Oh? Why?"

"Because it would ruin Warren Williams' plans and, possibly, his day." She hung up and called Helena and Isabella to come in to organize the next, and final, meeting with Drew Ryan.

"Ah, Helena and Isabella, there you are," Viola said when they arrived an hour later. "I just talked to Titania and the subject came up. Did you, by chance, kill some people in a..." Viola consulted her notes, "...some kind of hamburger restaurant in Pasadena?"

"Yes ma'am." Helena put down her purse and sat next to the window. She said hello to Kate, who poured her some tea.

"And did you also crash two tour buses?" Viola asked, consulting her notes again. "One into an intersection that continued into a car dealership, and the other, also into an intersection, but this one crashed into a shopping center, the, uh–" A quick look at her notes, "Paseo something?"

"Yessum," Isabella said, coming out of the bathroom, rubbing lotion into her hands.

"Ah, brava, then. Titania was a little annoyed, but she was fine by the end of the conversation," Viola said, and got sulky shrugs from the Americans and a sly smile from Kate. "By the way, my dears, there's a very bad cell phone photo of Helena, but only her closest friends would recognize her in it."

"I told you we should have killed everyone," Isabella said, wearily.

Helena looked annoyed. "We killed most of them, but there's no way we could confiscate all their cell phones."

"True," Isabella agreed.

"You shot the photographer, but he or she managed to take the picture while dying," Kate said.

"How heroic." Helena's tired sneer ended the conversation.

"Helena," Kate said, handing her an iPhone. "Any

idea who bloke this is?"

"That ain't a good shot of him, but I believe his name is Bishop," she said, looking closely. "He was in the jailhouse with Drew. Cellmate and protector. Used to walk him back to the cellblock from his therapy sessions. Never saw him in therapy, though."

"So now two of his jail friends have paid him a visit," Kate said. "Why?"

"He's cute? They wanna fuck him? Damn if I know." Helena was very tired. They were low on guns and ammo and she'd spent the day robbing gun stores. It was a tedious chore, but she had a trunk full of fun in the parking garage.

"He's dead," Viola said flatly.

"Who?" Helena asked.

"Ryan."

"When?" Isabella asked, surprised.

"Tomorrow, after we kill him," Viola told her.

"Unwise. I still think we can get the information out of the little bastard," Helena said. "As his jail shrink, I learned he talks when you scare him."

"We have jabs, we could bag him at his place tomorrow," Kate suggested.

"We could try, Viola," Isabella said. "I don't like giving up on this. Not after everything we've gone through."

Viola looked at three of the only six women, six human beings, in the world she trusted enough to turn her back on and, reluctantly, agreed to kidnap Ryan the next day.

After the strange events and very good tea at the Huntington, Drew found himself at loose ends again. Housework was still the most satisfying pastime he could indulge in alone. Masturbation led to dangerous thoughts of Reid, Bishop, and Samsa. Even the internet felt shallow or dangerous or just plain boring. He was only truly at peace in Russek's arms, and with the National Guard phasing themselves out of the city, he was seeing less and less of Russek.

But there was dust everywhere and dust always and Drew was dusting for all he was worth. Very meticulous, he removed all the objects from a surface, gave it a wipe with a dust grabbing cloth he bought at Smart & Final, then, depending on the surface, either washed it with Simple Green, or if it was wood, several coats of Old English Lemon Oil that he let soak in before wiping the residue off. Both of those products were also purchased at Smart & Final. He was well known at Smart and Final: clerks were recommending products to him.

Working clockwise around the living room, Drew had nearly convinced himself that his mind was a blank, focused completely on the task of dusting, polishing, wiping. This was something he'd read in the book on Zen Paul bought him at the Huntington after tea. In this calm and focused state, Drew was sure his worries and fears were melting away and that a new and better life, a life with Paul, a happy life with Paul, was coming closer and closer and closer...

And then, when he turned over the chummy photo of John Reid and Paul Russek on the mantle, Drew's mind really did go blank. He was momentarily blind and waves of hot and cold rolled through his body. Grasping the mantelpiece to stay upright, he looked in absolute horror at the photo of the man he loved and the man he thought he loved and he wasn't sure anymore which was which, or if they were even the same.

Dropping the photo, he staggered to the couch and sat heavily. After a few moments with his head between his knees, Drew attained a new level of clarity and knew he needed to talk to someone. Bishop was his first choice, but he had no way of contacting the man. There was Samsa and the cell phone Samsa gave him. Lunging for his computer bag, Drew prayed the man would answer, please answer, please answer, plea–

"Drew?" Samsa's voice was sweet in the earpiece.

"Samsa! Samsa! I've got to talk to you right

away!" Drew cried in relief and panic.

"I'll come–"

"No! Not here! Not here!" Drew ignored Samsa trying to calm him. "Meet me, um, meet me..." his eye fell on a postcard for a show he sort of wanted to see and he fixed his mind on that. "Meet me at the Los Angeles County Museum of Art!"

"Where?"

"The Los Ang–"

"Yeah, there, but where there? It's a big place."

"Oh." Drew took a breath and consulted the postcard. "Meet me at the, um, 'Phantom Sightings: Art after the Chicano Movement' exhibit. I'm leaving right now!" He hung up and rushed to Russek's car and nearly hit a motorcycle in his haste.

"That little bastard," Kate said under her helmet as she followed him. At a stop light she called Viola to tell her Ryan was on the move. Viola already knew from Titania and Miranda and gave her directions to the Los Angeles County Museum of Art. She and the Americans would meet her there.

"Fuck, where he going?" Bishop twisted in the driver's seat to watch Drew driving off and get a look at Lopez in the backseat. Whatever Lopez might be thinking was obscured by huge dark glasses.

"Follow him."

Russek got two calls almost simultaneously. One was that his car was heading southeast and the other was that the surveillance team heard Drew setting up a meeting with someone named Samsa at the LA County Museum of Art. "Sounds like you're in for a cultural afternoon, Russek," the desk sergeant told him when he relayed the information.

He was delayed by arresting a purse snatcher and then taking him to the hospital. The little old lady the kid mugged shot him with a Glock 9 mm and was claiming it was self-defense. Arresting her at the same time slowed him down, too. After turning everything over to another officer at the LA County Trauma Unit, Russek was finally able to head west to LACMA.

Samsa was late. Too restless to go inside and look at art, Drew paced around in front of the Art of the Americas building. He bought a latte and burned his mouth trying to drink it. He went to the bathroom— twice—and paced restlessly between the Ahmanson Building and the Pavilion of Japanese Art. Finally Samsa arrived, apologizing for traffic.

Carefully looking Drew over, Samsa sighed and pulled the kid into his arms. "You're not okay, are ya?" he asked.

"No," Drew said returning the embrace. "Not at all." Stepping back enough to reach into his pocket, he showed Samsa the picture and gave him a rough sketch of who John Reid was, who Paul Russek was, and why he was so upset they were in the same picture.

Samsa patted him on the back and drew him toward the escalator behind the old ticket booth. They were getting stares and he wanted more privacy. Also, if Drew became hysterical, which seemed likely, he didn't want an audience. "Where's this John Reid now?" he asked, smiling and waving at the museum guard's welcoming look.

"I don't know," Drew said, calmer now that he was tucked away in a corner with a view of the patio below. "He left me for the cops in the building we were robbing."

"The DARPA building."

"Yeah, how'd you know?"

"Rumors," Samsa said vaguely. "Where's Russek?"

"I don't know," Drew said, looking around, feeling nervous. "But he knows I'm here, the car is LoJohned–"

"Jacked, LoJacked," Samsa corrected him.

"Jacked, yeah, whatever," Drew said, starting to

Ginger Mayerson

panic again. "But what am I going to do? Samsa, help me, what am I going to do?"

Samsa put his arm around him. "Shhhh, don't worry," he whispered. "Don't worry, I'll keep ya safe." He barely heard a soft click, Drew's gasp, and then a knife slid between Samsa's ribs. He turned enough to see the museum guard's face. "You!"

Isabella pulled her knife out of Samsa and took a swing at Drew with the tranquillizer jab. She couldn't miss; she only had one left after the one she used to get the ugly guard uniform. Unfortunately, she did miss, but the jab was still full. She was in a better position and Ryan was frozen in front of her.

"Drew!"

She turned from Ryan to see Russek running up the escalator at her. She threw the knife which pierced his leather jacket very near his neck, and she bolted back into the museum.

"Drew! Are you okay?" Russek was torn between pain, fear, and the serious need to kick the shit out of one knife-throwing old woman. He noticed Samsa bleeding next to Drew. "Hey, you're that guy–"

"That's one of the Sirens," Samsa gasped out. "One of the terrorists trying to kill Drew! Go. Get. Her!"

"I'm okay, go!" Drew gave him a panicky, but reassuring look. As Russek ran after Isabella, Drew saw another female museum guard coming up the escalator. But this guard had a gun and it was aimed at Russek's back. Drew got between her and the gun. "No!"

"You little fucking idiot," Helena snarled, putting her gun away, and getting her own jab out. She'd finish off Samsa after Ryan was down. Drew nearly fell over Samsa as she moved in. His gasp tipped her off that she should look behind her.

"Bishop!" Drew yelled.

"Goddammit!" Helena swung with the jab, which gave her enough time grab her gun. It was a point-blank shot, except Drew shoved her arm so Bishop could

178

knock the gun out of her hand.

It was hand-to-hand combat then. Helena had commando training in the Army and was the best fighter of any of them, but Bishop had at least fifty pounds and several inches on her. That left hand-to-hand swamp rat fighting technique, and she was good at that, too. She kicked him in the balls and punched him on the side of his throat. He went down like a sack of potatoes.

Real museum guards and security were running towards them. Helena screamed for help and ran across the bridge and into the Art of the Americas building. Inside, she shed her museum guard coat and put on the scarf she had in her pocket. She knew she was done there, so she moved to a safe place to watch from. She didn't know where Viola was, but she dearly hoped Kate was on the motorcycle backing up Isabella, because there was nothing she could do just then to help her.

Isabella knew she wasn't as sophisticated as Viola, or educated as Kate, or as good a hand-to-hand fighter as Helena, but she could run like a motherfucker and that was exactly what she was doing at that moment. She was, in fact, completely focused on running at top speed through the long galleries between the Hammer and Ahmanson buildings. To panic the crowds in the galleries, she shot several museum-goers and jumped over their bodies. She thought she heard Russek slipping in their blood or tripping over their bodies, and that bought her a little time. He wasn't shooting at her, but he must have his gun drawn because she could hear people yelling, "Don't shoot the art!" This almost drowned out his yelling, "Stop that bitch!" Which no one did because they were all diving for cover.

There were sirens. "Dammit," she thought taking the stairs to the ground floor two at a time while turning her museum guard coat inside out and putting it back on. She let her hair down and tied the scarf in her pocket around her head. She couldn't do anything about her skirt or how much she now looked like a harmless babushka. At least she hoped she looked harmless.

The crowds between the Ahmanson and the Broad buildings were curious about the fire trucks, ambulances, and police cars roaring down Wilshire, but not panicked. Isabella moved with them towards the Broad building. Behind her, she could hear Russek getting lots of shit for examining the women in his path. She looked around for Kate or Helena, but neither were visible. To avoid Russek, she rode the escalator to the third level with the rest of the conceptual art lovers.

Slipping quietly down to the second level, she saw Russek entering from the outside stairs. She retreated back into the Damien Hirst exhibit of dead things. She wasn't sure of the layout, but she thought it might be a circle and he'd be behind her very soon. Moving toward the front doors, she got her gun out, but kept it concealed as she exchanged smiles with the real museum guard, who was giving her an odd look. Russek's heavy steps preceded him (why are men so loud? she wondered for the nth time), and she made her decision, which turned out to be the wrong one. She shot at him and missed. Then she shot the dead sheep tank. Formaldehyde gushed out over the floor. Russek took a shot at her as she flashed out the door. Over the guard's hysterical screaming, she heard, more than saw, him slip in the formaldehyde behind her.

Tossing off her jacket and dragging the scarf around her neck, Isabella found her way blocked by police and had no choice but to run into the ground floor gallery. The only things in it were huge steel walls she would later learn were by some guy named Serra with a metal fetish. She played cat and mouse in them with the cops until one of the sculptures fell down from being shot so much. She was running to the one on the other side, when machine gun fire from outside shattered all the windows facing Wilshire. She ran towards it and found Kate on a motorcycle under the windows. She jumped on and they roared down Wilshire with, seemingly, half of the LAPD in pursuit.

They rode into the first large indoor shopping center they came to, shoplifted some new clothes, tripped the fire alarms, and got away in the ensuing confusion.

"What a bloody disaster," Kate observed as they drove away in a carjacked Lexus.

"You're telling me, darlin'?" Isabella said as they drove past the continuing chaos at the museum. "And you didn't have to look at fucked-up dead animals and industrial materials art either."

They picked up Helena at the Marie Callenders near the La Brea Tar Pits and asked about Viola. "Dunno, but let's not go too far in case she needs us." It was lunchtime anyway, so they got a table and ordered salads.

As Russek was chasing Isabella through the galleries between the buildings, Viola was peacefully gazing at one of her most favorite paintings in the world: *The Magdalen with the Smoking Flame*, by George de la Tour. It was such a profound painting of a woman, deep in thought holding a skull in her lap, and all in such unspeakably beautiful candlelight. One could almost feel the light on the woman's bare shoulders as she meditated on flame beside her. As Viola was meditating on the painting and trying to ignore the incredible mess unfolding behind her, she could almost feel the darkness sidling up on her right.

"Quite brilliant, that painting, eh, Mademoiselle?" Williams opened conversationally.

"Yes."

"Any idea whose skull that is?"

"No."

"We're neither of us succeeding here, are we?"

"Succeeding at what?" Viola asked, turning her head a millimeter in his direction.

"Succeeding at getting Drew Ryan, of course."

"I only want what he stole from us," she said, omitting the "At your behest" part.

"Of course, that's what I want, too," Williams said

blandly staring at the painting. "But I want the boy as well. Don't you?"

"No."

"Oh, come now, Mademoiselle. Even you found him charming enough to take to bed."

"I was bored," she said, gently patting her brow with her hand. "What was your excuse?"

"That you found him charming enough to take to bed."

"Only that?"

"Yes."

"If that was all, then you really are an idiot, Warren," she said disinterestedly.

"It was at first," Williams said, matching her tone. "But now I want him."

She looked him full in the face.

"And I also want what he stole from you," he added. He tensed as she reached into her pocket.

"Just getting a, ah, mouchoir." She held up a large lacy object. "What do you call it?"

"Handkerchief, I guess," he said relaxing fractionally.

"Ah, yes, please excuse me," she said, bringing the handkerchief to her forehead and swaying a little. "It's quite dreadful, these, these, les bouffées de chaleur, what do you call–?"

"Hot flashes?"

"Yes, very...oh!" She swayed into him and he caught her. She clicked open the switchblade hidden in the lace hanky and slid it into his side. She knew her angle was bad for a kill, but it was the thought that counted.

"Oh, damn!" he hissed, dragging her to the floor with him. He wrenched at her wrist to get her to let go of the knife, which she did.

Getting free of him, Viola rose and said, dramatically that she'd go for help, even as men in EMT jumpsuits were on their way over to them. She exchanged a wry look with Williams, who was very busy holding the knife to keep it from doing any more damage to his torso.

She left him there as the sirens reached a crescendo outside. Also helpful was the woman who caught sight of the blood seeping from Williams' side and screamed, thus starting all the women screaming. Viola used this as cover to slip out of the gallery, down the stairs and around the back of the buildings, and leave the museum via the La Brea Tar Pits entrance. Once away from the police and sirens, she called Kate and joined them for lunch at Marie Callenders. At that moment, eating was the last thing on her mind, so she only had a coffee.

"Not hungry, Vi?" Helena teased.

"You'd have no appetite if you'd just heard what I did," she said.

"What?" they asked.

"Williams thinks he's in love with Ryan."

"Ew!" And none of them could finish their lunches. They needed to get a move on anyway before it occurred to the LAPD to start looking for witnesses in the area.

At the hospital, Russek was only slightly surprised to see Agents Romero and Carpenter of the DHS and the FBI respectively stroll into the Cedars-Sinai emergency room. Russek was bravely trying to make sense of what Drew and Bishop were telling him about what would later be called the LACMA Incident. Samsa was still getting stitched up and the nurses were keeping everyone out.

"I hope you've got some fucking answers, because a lot of people died today," Russek snarled, glad to have a target he could hate with impunity.

"We're looking for answers, too, Russek," Romero assured him.

Carpenter merely looked grim. "I think a few answers just walked in," he said, nodding toward a suit having a word with a hospital administrator suit behind the nursing station.

Their stare must have gotten his attention, because the suit turned and exchanged nods with Romero and Carpenter and raked his eyes over the other three, lingering on Drew. He had another word with the hospital suit, and then strolled over to their group.

"You're early," he said affably to Romero and Carpenter. "I was hoping to look in on my man, but he's still knocked out, so let's have our chat. All of us." He gestured for them to follow him. They were joined by the hospital suit, who led them to an empty office and left them there.

Once inside, the suit handed out business cards with the CIA's logo on them.

"Josef Schweik," Drew said slowly. "You guys must think no one reads Czech fiction. Josef Schweik, is 'The Good Soldier Schweik.' Not as famous as Gregor Samsa, but still fiction."

"Yeah," Russek said, hoping Drew was right. "Who the fuck are you?"

"He's CIA," Carpenter answered Russek. "That's all we need to know."

"That Samsa guy CIA, too?" Bishop asked.

"Yes," Schweik said. "And a damn good agent."

"He was a bad mutherfucker in the jailhouse," Bishop said blandly.

"It was necessary," Schweik told him and turned to the group. "You don't know what you're dealing with here. Carpenter and Romero have some idea, but you've seen what the Sirens can do. You've been seeing it for weeks."

"Sirens...Samsa yelled that at me," Russek said. "'Get her, she's a Siren,' I think."

Drew nodded. "Yeah. Wha–?"

"A terrorist organization," Schweik cut him off. "And you're right in the middle of it, Mr. Ryan."

"Not because I want to be, Mr. 'Schweik'," Drew shot back.

"Look, you three are all about terrorism," Russek said, pulling Drew behind him. "Can't you catch these people?"

"Of course," Schweik said, looking down his nose at the LAPD detective. "And we will...eventually. Right now this is the biggest, most brutal assault we've had from them on U.S. soil."

"What about Irvine?" Drew asked. "You know they did that, don't you?"

Schweik smiled a little too confidently "Of course we know that," he said, waving his hand dismissively. "We–"

"You didn't know that, didja, tough guy?" Bishop asked menacingly. "Don't act like ya did, asshole, I can tell when cops like you are lying." He turned to Drew. "He was lying."

Drew nodded, and mouthed, "I know."

"We," Romero slid in, "at the DHS, thought the Sirens, or one of them, was responsible for the Irvine incident." He inclined his head at Drew. "Thank you for the confirmation. However incriminating."

"Now wait a minute," Russek said, sounding deadly. "You're not going to hang this and that mess on Drew. I'll–"

"No. We're not." Schweik's cold voice could have cut through Richard Serra's toppled iron walls back at the LACMA gallery. "We need Mr. Ryan's help to catch the Sirens, if we can."

"This 'Siren' name is new to me," Carpenter said, reminding them of his existence. "We haven't seen them as a unit. More as individuals with a central command."

"Our intelligence," Schweik paused to let Bishop finish his mirthless laugh, "indicates they are that, but also work as a unit. We have been trying to connect them with the Irvine incident, but only one or two of them. We have no idea how many are in Los Angeles, we can only account for two, but the volume of terror would indicate at least a dozen."

"Two? You've got leads on two? Why haven't you–?" Russek began.

"Because the two we think we can identify are supposed to be dead." Schweik pulled some photos out of his briefcase and handed them around. "Recognize either of them?"

"I think..." Drew was frowning and staring hard. "I think, I don't know. These are younger women than I met."

"We've found prints in Los Angeles for Rosella Martin of New Orleans," Schweik said, pointing to an unsmiling woman in a uniform. "This photo is from her Army file. She received an honorable discharge in 2005, she disappeared after Katrina, and then her fingerprints were found in the debris of an explosion in Jackson, Florida. Officially, she's dead. Unofficially, she's been at or near dozens of terrorists incidents all over the world over the past year and a half."

"If she was the woman at the museum, she fight like a mutherfucker," Bishop said.

"She should. She was combat trained."

Bishop shrugged. "Well, that explains everything."

Schweik shrugged, too, and held another photo up for Drew. "Recognize her from Baku?" he asked and Drew shook his head. "You should. Our reliable sources there say you spent the night in a Baku whorehouse with her."

"She was older," Drew said, hastily adding, "than that picture."

"We think this woman's name is Yasmin Khoury," Schweik said. "The French security types are being very cagey about who she is and what she used to do for them. We think the French External Security organization loaned her out to NATO or the Arab League or something as a killer in Russia, Central Asia, and the Middle East. We had to steal this information after Interpol admitted we had her fingerprints and pointed us to the parts of the French Foreign Ministry that technically don't exist."

"Were they spies?" Drew asked.

"Not for us." Schweik gathered up the picture.

"Martin was a model soldier. The Army was sorry to lose her, but fighting in Iraq soured her on the whole deal. We know nothing about Khoury except her name and her fingerprints from the French External Security organization, and this picture we think is of her. We suspect she's Middle Eastern, but who knows? She could be anything."

"And the others?" Carpenter, who was less informed than Romero, prompted.

"No fingerprint match-ups," Schweik said. "If they're from a nation hostile to the U.S.–"

"That's a lot," Bishop quipped.

Schweik ignored him. "–they're not going to help us. We blew up the records in Baghdad and Kabul, and Israel took out the Palestinian Authority records—not that the Palestinians would help us anyway—so we've got zip. And, as Mr. Bishop might know, the U.S. doesn't fingerprint its law-abiding citizens unless they request it. So if there are American Sirens, we don't have anything on record to identify them with."

"How you know my name?" Bishop asked.

"Samsa went into great detail about what a bad mutherfucker you are, Mr. Bishop," Schweik said.

"Sirens," Drew said thoughtfully.

"Yeah, Sirens," Russek snarled. "If you three government hotshots have all this information and terrorist fighting machinery, why can't you catch these broads?"

"Many reasons, Detective," Schweik said, officiously. "Because they're lucky, ruthless, lethal, but most of all because they blend into their environment and no one can remember what they look like. Can you? Can any of you remember any of the middle-aged women you've met recently well enough to describe her and identify her?" They all shook their heads. "So you see what we're up against: ruthless, intelligent, sophisticated, middle-aged, Westernized women with money and bleeding-edge technology behind them."

"And luck," Bishop added.

"Yes, and luck," Schweik affirmed. "Luck like the devil."

There seemed to be nothing else to say, so the little group broke up. The civil servants went off to their own discussions as Russek offered Bishop a ride back to the Museum parking garage.

In the car, Russek said, "I really hope those guys in there are lying about how little they know about these Sirens—"

"Because if they not lying and they really that stupid," Bishop continued for him. "We completely fucked."

"Yeah," Drew said softly.

In another part of the Emergency Room, Williams was signing himself out against medical advice. Even his attorney, who'd nearly had to threaten a lawsuit to get him out, was dubious.

"Really, Mr. Lopez," Orselli said, recoiling from the bloody bandages on his boss' side. "Don't you think—"

"No, I don't. Get the car." Williams knew he'd been lucky that Mademoiselle's knife hadn't gone very deep or very straight, but he'd still bled a lot and been in a lot of pain. He hadn't been able to get away from the helpful crowd that insisted he go to the hospital with the paramedics. In a normal situation, Williams would have been grateful to the good citizens of Los Angeles, but this was far from a normal situation. "And get this thing filled." He shoved a prescription for painkillers and antibiotics at Orselli as they drove back to his safe house downtown. And then he passed out, but later insisted it was just a nap.

Chapter 13

Here Lie Love's Undiscover'd Mines

"Sirens?" Titania marveled at the word. "I never knew that's what they called us."

"It's not exactly a compliment, Agent Titania," the Department Manager said.

"Schweik came very close to identifying two of your operatives. Doesn't that worry you?" her Section Manager asked with a snarl.

"I would worry if they caught them and then identified them," Titania said serenely.

Her Section Manager snorted rudely and excused himself. He went into the bathroom.

Titania and the Department Manager sat in silence, looking blandly across the table at each other. Then the Department Manager took a package of white powder from his coat, took the lid off the Section Manager's latte, stirred the powder into it, and replaced the lid.

Returning to his seat, her Section Manager took a big swig of his latte and asked her, "Your people have traumatized two Los Angeles cultural institutions and an archdiocese. What do you have to say for yourself?"

She looked into his dangerously purple face and said, "Nothing."

"Nothing!? Eruk!" Her Section Manager fell face first onto the table with a solid, though squishy, thump.

Titania gazed at the Department Manager, waiting for the next move.

"You never did answer him," he said gently.

"It seemed like it would be a waste of time," she said, also gently.

"What do you have to say for yourself, Agent Titania?" he asked.

She sighed. "Sometimes the destination is more important than the journey. But they never tell that to the kids and the suckers of the world."

"Why not?"

"They'd kill everyone they could find if they knew how pointless it all really is."

Because Viola loathed driving and didn't do it very well anyway, Kate, Helena, and Isabella kept watch on Russek's house. They noticed the bland cars, mostly unadorned silver Toyota Corollas, also watching Russek's house. They relayed the license plates to Miranda as they saw them. There were only five cars in rotation; Titania assumed this was due to the CIA budget being shifted away from Los Angeles and to the unrest fomenting in other parts of the country due to the economic meltdown. If sabots were going to be thrown into looms, no doubt the CIA would want to be on the ground floor of something they could, maybe, handle. Titania knew it was the CIA because they did a bad job covering their tracks on the rental cars they were using. She had all the information she needed after running and tracing the license plates the team in LA relayed to her. The CIA was also stupid in that the rentals were LoJacked and easy to follow once Miranda had their signal.

"I wonder how many marriages LoJack has ruined," Miranda mused one morning.

"I wonder how many it's saved," Titania mused back at her. "A man behaves a little differently when he knows he might get caught."

"What about women?"

"They're too smart to get caught." Titania sipped her coffee and looked at her coded to-do list. "Speaking of marriages, what's going on in the Russek-Ryan romance?"

"They're not talking about anything important where the microphones are. I highlighted the stuff I thought was odd, but not crucial." Miranda handed her a summary of their conversations and phone calls. "We need more staff for this kind of operation. Like, we need some staff for this kind of operation."

"Like, we need to get out of this operation, because we're not staffed for it. Or good at it. Luckily or unluckily it's the only thing we're working on these days," Titania added, scanning the list. "What's this one-sided conversation for Ryan last week? Looks like he tried to call Samsa and got a flunky. This is the second call to Samsa, isn't it?"

"Yes. He has a cell phone we don't have access to," Miranda said. "I tried to get something on it when he called Samsa before the LACMA thing," she paused to let Titania grimace, and continued, "But I couldn't dig anything up on it. I asked Viola what the chances are of getting a look at it and she said the chances are nonexistent. She was in a bad mood."

"She has a lot to be in a bad mood about," Titania said, re-skimming the list. "They're stuck in LA, spinning their wheels. Did you find anything about the phone?"

"No. He's only used it twice, both times to call Samsa."

"When? Before or after Samsa's visit?" Titania asked, flipping through the previous surveillance data. "After," she said, answering her own question. "Samsa gave him that phone. It's a CIA phone. And a CIA phone would have lots of things in it."

"Like a tracking device?"

"Which is how Samsa got to the Huntington when no one was watching the house until now," Titania said.

"Why is the CIA watching the house now?" Miranda asked. She knew the DHS and FBI were under-funded on this mission because their bosses didn't think it was important. That decision was based on information Miranda fed into their databases. Romero and Carpenter were real-world experience guys and knew what they were up against even if their bosses didn't.

"They're hoping we'll show up so they can kill us. We've hurt one of their own and embarrassed them. That annoys them very much," Titania said, thoughtfully. "They're under-funded, too, but they keep a file open on us, and with Samsa out of commission, they must have someone new running things. Whoever that is might have an agenda beyond Ryan and the data he stole. Even though we've covered our financial tracks, which is the most important thing, we still need to know what he got. There's not much else of interest he could have, um, hacked? Is that the word?"

"Yes. And yes, our financial tracks are so covered, you and I couldn't even trace them if we didn't know what we were looking for," Miranda said with a groan. She hated being reminded of the horrible mess she, in part, had caused. "But we still need to know what he stole and get whatever he put it on back." She held up her hand to stave off Titania's hopeful question. "And, yes, I'm sure it's not on the internet. I would have found it by now. Ryan isn't that smart–"

"But Williams is."

"But he's not internet savvy," Miranda said, with a small smile. "Williams is old school and proud of it. I think that's why he glommed onto Ryan the way he did." She watched Titania nod. "And if Ryan put it on the internet, I would have found it because I know how Ryan thinks better than he does. Or how he used to think. I think he's changed."

"Y'think? Why?" Titania looked away from her paperwork and down at Miranda.

"Because Helena told me that Ryan got between her gun and Russek's back at the museum," Miranda said slowly. "And the Klaarance I knew in Electricland wouldn't have done that for anyone."

"Don't call him Klaarance," Titania said, tiding the file and handing it back to Miranda. "It gives me the creeps when you call Ryan that."

"I won't call him Klaarance anymore, Titania," Miranda said sweetly. "Because Klaarance is dead and

I'm not sure what we're dealing with in this Ryan kid now."

Viola had been thinking hard about many things in the days after the failed grab at the museum. Mostly that they were running out of time and resources, and the element of surprise was all but gone.

She called her colleagues together and outlined her plan. "We'll need C4 and possibly your Samoan girls for a diversion."

"Samoans we have, but C4 we're out of," Kate told her with regret.

"Get some," Viola said, sternly. "Improvise. All of you, to work! This is our last chance. We must succeed."

They scattered, leaving Viola to make arrangements with Titania and Miranda.

The email from Bishop had been short and sweet: "Gallodrome in 1 hour. Bring nothing."

Drew emailed back: "Should I wear clothes?" But there was no answer, so he took a shower and drove down to the Gallodrome to meet Bishop an hour later. Once his eyes adjusted to the gloom, he looked around, but didn't see Bishop. The bartender caught his eye and jerked his chin at a very, very dark corner, which was where Bishop was. Drew walked up to the table and said, "Hi."

Bishop said, "Let's go." Outside, Bishop handed him a clunky helmet and put on a smaller one himself. "They're ugly, but I don't want to fight with the cops right now. Hop on."

Swinging his leg over the chopper, Drew put his arms around Bishop's waist. Bishop didn't seem to mind. "Where are we going?" he asked, but the engine was loud and they were getting on the freeway, so he didn't think Bishop heard him.

They rode down the freeway and pulled off into an industrial area, twisting and winding deep into it until

Drew had lost all sense of direction. Bishop pulled into a warehouse loading bay and pulled his helmet off. "We're going here," he said, smirking.

Drew leaned forward to kiss him, but Bishop pulled back and led him into the gloomy cavernous space. They took a freight elevator up three floors and stepped out into an equally huge space lit by giant windows and skylights. Dazzled, Drew could only clutch at Bishop's jacket and follow him. They crossed the space and went into an office space sketched out with walls, but no ceilings. An effeminate sharply-dressed man rose at their entrance and disappeared into another room and returned with John Reid.

Jerking back, Drew found himself held against Bishop's rock solid physique. "You!" Drew hissed, shaking like a leaf. His knees were so weak, Bishop was mostly holding him up.

Slowly, never taking his eyes off Drew's face, Williams-Reid-Lopez crossed the space between them and cupped Drew's jaw to raise his eyes to him. "Drew," he said gently, like a prayer, softly stroking the young man's cheeks.

Somewhat soothed, or at least enough to trust his voice, "What are you doing here, John?" he asked, completely missing the look Bishop and Orselli exchanged.

It was not lost on Williams, who pulled Drew into his arms and glared at his, or rather Lopez's, employees. "Did you think I'd left you? How could you think that?" he asked against the top of Drew's head. This was awkward because Drew was trying to squirm away from him. Firmly holding Drew at arms length, Williams fixed him with his most powerful man-quieting stare. "I love you, Drew," he said, his voice dripping with profound emotion. "I'd never leave you."

Speechless, Drew went very still and put his arms around Williams when the man held him close. He turned his face up and allowed himself to be passionately kissed. "But now what?" Drew asked after a few moments of his face buried in Williams' chest. When he looked up, they were alone in the room.

"Well, we finish the job and get out of town," Williams said softly. "And we'll have the life I promised you. We'll–" Williams looked around. "What was that?" he asked, stepping away from Drew.

"What was what?" Drew asked.

Jerking the door open, Williams barely had time yell for Bishop before the shooting started downstairs. "Get him out of here!" He shoved Drew at Bishop and led them and Orselli down a flight of stairs at the back of the offices.

Outside, Williams and Orselli vanished. Drew and Bishop got halfway around the building before they were surrounded. They were brought at gunpoint to Schweik and Samsa.

"Samsa!" Drew blurted out. "You're okay?"

"Yeah, I'm okay," Samsa said neutrally, keeping an eye on Bishop. He told his people to lower their guns. "What are you doing here, Drew?"

Schweik suggested they sit in the back of limousine, but they left Bishop outside. "Well?" he asked.

"Williams was here," Drew said coming clean. "He wanted me to leave with him."

"Would you?"

"No."

Looking skeptical, Schweik murmured, "Then we were just in time."

"How did you know I was here?" Drew asked Samsa.

"We had a lead on Williams," Samsa said quickly. "Anything else happen, Drew?"

"No."

"What's Bishop doing here?" Samsa asked.

"I think he works with Williams," Drew said slowly. "Let's ask him." They got out of the limo and found a very annoyed Bishop.

"He called himself Lazarus Lopez," Bishop said,

exasperated. "He was the new boss of our organization when I got out of jail. I'm just a gofer, man, a Drew-delivery boy, that's all."

Schweik and Samsa stepped out of earshot and had a small argument before they came back and told Bishop he could go. They offered Drew a ride back to Silverlake, but he decided to ride back with Bishop.

"You know how to find me," Samsa said gently. "Don't worry about anything, we're very close to catching the bastard," he added when Drew frowned and lowered his eyes.

"Will you tell Paul about this?" Drew asked, adding, "Paul Russek," when Samsa looked confused.

"Not if you don't want me to," he said.

"No, not yet," Drew said, suspecting Samsa, with his improved grammar and diction, would do as he pleased no matter what pleased Drew.

Climbing onto Bishop's motorcycle, the cell phone from Samsa pressed against Drew's thigh in the pocket he'd forgotten he had it in.

Once again Bishop was silent on the ride back to where Drew had parked Russek's car. "What you going to do, Drew?" he demanded once Drew had his helmet off.

"I don't know." Drew stared hard at him. "I don't know who I can trust anymore. I thought you–"

"Leave me out of it," Bishop snapped. "Or let me tell you this: I'm on your side. I didn't keep 'em off you in the lockup for you, or for me, I mostly did it for Russek." He looked coldly at Drew. "So if you going to fuck Russek over, you have to get past me to do it." He softened a little. "Hey, Drew, I didn't know Lopez was this Williams mutherfucker. If Samsa hadn't crashed in, I woulda killed him."

"You would?" Drew swayed toward him.

"Sure." Bishop pulled him into his arms and welded his mouth onto Drew's. He was equal parts sorry and glad they were in an open air parking lot so things couldn't go any further. Pushing Drew away, he promised to come to Russek's that night to figure out what they were all going to do. "Go home, Drew, stay there until Russek gets there."

"I will, I just need to do some grocery shopping first," Drew said, jerking his thumb at the market behind them. "Where will you be?"

"Beating some answers out of a certain shyster lawyer," Bishop said darkly and then rode off.

Drew watched him go and then turned to go into the market. He shrugged, cleared his mind for grocery shopping and strolled into the store. Near the frozen food case at the back of the store, a woman he recognized two seconds too late sidled up to him and the world went black.

"Oh, these silly drunks," Viola said to the passing stock clerk who was helping her get Drew into the shopping cart. "Would you mind helping me get him into my car? It's behind the store."

The clerk was perfectly happy to help the lovely woman with the charming accent and gracious smile put her drunken son into the giant Winnebago behind the store.

On the way to the freeway, Bishop passed a Winnebago being driven by a woman who looked vaguely familiar. Being paranoid made a man good at faces, but no one had asked him about the Sirens or offered to let him identify one. It would have been a waste of his valuable sociopathic time anyway. But a little further on he saw a smashed up car and a crowd around it. He slowed down enough to look inside. There was a revolving red light, just like a cop would have in an unmarked cop car. Before he'd consciously put it together, he'd wheeled his chopper and was following the Winnebago, which was like a singlewide mobile home on wheels, so it was easy to follow.

The recreational vehicle drove into the market parking lot Bishop had just left Drew in and pulled around the back of the market, where there was another RV. "What the fuck is this? A convention?" Bishop asked himself, but never got an answer because the RVs headed out.

He followed them down Glendale Boulevard where they were obeying the speed limit, but sped up to make a light. Bishop had to gun it to make the same light, which, in retrospect, was stupid because he could see these RVs for miles. The RV in front of him slammed on its brakes and Bishop slammed into the back of it. That was the last thing he remembered of being on his motorcycle. Well, almost the last; the very last was a middle-aged woman bending over him and a sharp jab in his neck. Then the world clicked off like a men's room light on a timer.

Some nice motorists stopped and helped Kate get Bishop into Helena's RV. Then Helena headed east and Isabella went north.

After cuffing and gagging the unconscious Bishop, Kate sat in the passenger seat, working on Drew's cell phone per Miranda's detailed instructions on misdirecting the trackers. She looked over the road ahead of them. "This is like riding an elephant," she said, conversationally.

"When'd you ever ride an elephant?" Helena asked, pulling into the very busy parking lot of a cluster of big box stores.

"Never," Kate said. "And now I don't have to." She got out of her seat to check the webcam setup.

"You do a good job driving these big American cars."

Isabella tried not to blush from Viola's compliment.

"But of course cars like this are horrible, but they must be driven," Viola went on, moodily drinking her coffee. "So, if that is so, it's good if they are driven well."

Drew coming around saved Isabella from having to formulate an answer or simply look intelligent in her silence. She liked Viola very much, but didn't understand her more philosophical moods, which were becoming more frequent as the pressure increased on all of them.

"Oh no, oh no," he moaned and started yelling for help.

Viola brought the butt of her revolver down on his thigh and then tapped it on his fly as he gasped in pain. "You start yelling again, I use it here," tap tap, "and very hard, too."

Isabella glanced out the window. She'd pulled the RV into a parking lot in Alhambra, far enough away from anyone with super-hearing who might have heard what little noise escaped from it. She looked at Drew, duct-taped into his seat facing an open laptop, and thought, "Yell your fool head off, boy, there's no one to hear you anyway."

Sitting opposite Drew, Viola inhaled and smiled wistfully. "I should have just killed you in Baku," she said conversationally. "That's what I thought and I didn't. My mistake."

"You just wanted to seduce me," Drew said with touching nervous courage.

"No, I wanted to kill you after we had sex," Viola told him. She took a burnished metal rectangle out of her handbag and put it on the table within easy reach. "You're a terrible lover. Really, just dreadful." She shook her head as if to clear it. "But the past is the past and nothing can be done. We must live in the present and look to the future. You are making my present difficult, Drew, and I will not allow you to annoy me in the future. Where is the data you stole from us in the DARPA building? Give it to us and we let you go."

"I don't believe you," Drew said, his voice shaking. "That flash drive is all that's keeping me alive, isn't it?"

"Oh, it's on a flash drive, as you call it, good to know." Viola picked up the metal object on the table before her and clicked the blade open. "Would it be easier to tell me where this flash drive is if I cut off your little finger? Perhaps both little fingers?" she asked, not moving toward him. "Or, perhaps severing the tendons in the back of the hand so your fingers don't work, or don't work very well? And then there's genital mutilation, but I like to save that for last."

"I'd rather die," Drew said dramatically.

"Yes, that's preferable to losing everything you love and live for, isn't it? But you're not in charge of that decision; I am." She clicked the knife shut and looked at Isabella, who gave her a thumbs up. "Perhaps there is something you care about more," she said, pressing the laptop start button. "Perhaps it is someone you care about."

The screen came on of a man duct-taped in a chair very much like the one and the way Drew was restrained. The man had a black bag over his head and C4 with wires in it strapped around his waist. The bag was theatrically whipped off to show it was Russek, gagged, and blindfolded.

Drew's breath rushed out of him in a keening whine and he screwed his eyes shut. Viola slapped him hard. "Open your eyes," she commanded softly. "He's still alive. The man you love more than your own life. You, and only you, can save him now." She grabbed a handful of his hair and turned him to face her. He spat in her face. She brought the gun butt down on his nearest hand and he screamed. "You're really an idiot," she said, wiping his spittle off her face. "Killing you and Russek will be more pleasure than chore."

"But you'll let us go if I give you the flash drive," he said wildly.

"After you spat in my face?" Viola asked in a hurt voice.

Isabella cleared her throat.

"Oh, yes, thank you for the reminder," Viola said. She slowly closed the laptop. "Well, Drew, I'm not completely insane yet, and my colleague is a woman of honor, so she'll hold me to the deal we've made: you give me the flash drive with the data on it, and you swear this is all there is, and we will let you and Russek go." She met his dubious eye and raised her right hand. "As God is my witness."

After a few moments of silence, Drew told them the flash drive was in a desk leg in the DARPA building.

"Which desk?" Viola asked.

"Whichever one I was under during the firefight."

"Oh. Mon. Dieu."

"Oh, fuck." Miranda leaned back in her chair and gave Titania the bad news: The DARPA front had been closed since the firefight earlier in the year. It was still considered a police investigation scene, though Miranda couldn't find any references to it in the LAPD databases. She could find no cameras at or on the building, and only minimal electricity was running inside and out. There was a security patrol that drove by on a loose schedule that included the entire industrial park. She looked over at Titania studying a map and a floorplan. "We need time for a plan to–"

"We don't have any time," Titania said. "The team has three hostages, two stolen Winnebagos, and half a dozen Samoan girls ready for action. It's now and the data or nine dead bodies in the riverbed." She sighed and arched her aching back. "Get Viola on a secure line, please."

Viola looked at her notes and made a few more before calling Kate. "Bring your Samoans," she said. "They can help us turn over desks."

Kate left in the RV Drew had been in. Viola and Isabella moved him into the one with Russek and Bishop, but kept him hooded and gagged. Bishop was still knocked out, but handcuffed and firmly duct-taped into a swivel seat. They installed Drew in a facing seat and headed south, to the DARPA building.

It was dark when they got there. They faked a breakdown so the security patrol would find them and they could kill them and steal their car and their keys.

The first car that stopped was a young woman who offered to call Auto Club for them. Isabella assured her that they had already called Triple A and the tow truck was just a few minutes away. The girl offered to wait with her, but Helena stuck her head out and waved, and convinced the girl they'd be okay. Then next Samaritan was a middle-aged man who ended up in his own trunk for trying to be helpful.

"You know, there're some very nice people in Los Angeles," Viola observed as she helped Helena move the body.

"Yeah. Too bad for them."

Finally the security patrol showed up: it was one old guy who fit neatly in the trunk of the patrol car.

Viola drove the Samaritan's car; Isabella drove the patrol car. They found the locks already broken on the chain-link security fence and parked in the shadows behind the DARPA building. Kate was there waiting for them with six very focused, and heavily armed, Samoan girls.

Miranda had remotely disabled the alarm system so all that was left was to break in and start looking. They assigned two of the largest girls to steer Russek and the somewhat-conscious Bishop into the building with them. Viola jammed her gun into Drew's kidney and asked him where they should start.

"Un-blindfold Paul," Drew said, his teeth chattering in fear. "He might remember better."

"Yeah, maybe that cop memory is good for something," Helena said, wrapping a headscarf around her hair and lower part of her face.

The Samoan girls looked on with mild interest as the older women veiled their faces. Russek's sight and speech were restored, and his first words were, "Fuck, Drew, I was hoping they just got me." He noticed the hooded man next to him. "Is that Bishop?"

"Shut up, Russek!" Helena barked. "Where'd you find Ryan hereabouts?"

"Why?" Russek asked with a snarl.

"Because if you don't tell me I'm gonna shoot his hands until they're stumps," she waved the gun in that direction. "Then I'll work on his feet, then knees, then his dick, then—"

"Fuck! Stop! On the second floor," Russek said, quickly.

They found the stairs and on the second floor, Russek and Ryan could agree on the general area. The Samoan girls got to work overturning desks, and eventually they found the one desk with the flash drive jammed between the back leg and the desktop. Drew identified it as his.

The three men were shoved into decrepit desk chairs and the Samoan girls almost looked like they were having fun duct-taping them into them.

While they were doing that, Isabella positioned a webcam and a listening device discreetly near them. Kate activated the tracking device in the cell phone Samsa gave Drew and they all melted away with the Samoan girls.

"Wait for my signal," Kate said, getting into the RV with Viola, Helena, and Isabella. "You wait or I won't pay you the other half."

"We know the deal," Sina said. "Like you, we keep our word."

Kate stared at her for a moment. "Good luck."

"We don't need luck," Sina said, hoisting an AK47. "We got these."

As they drove away in the RV, they saw a silver Toyota parked the front of the DARPA building. "That was fast," Helena said.

"Too fast," Kate said, and logged the laptop into the webcam and microphones on the second floor. "I hope they don't mess up our plan."

"Our plan is finished," Viola said like slamming a steel door. "I don't care what they do. Please drive faster, Isabella."

"We don't need a ticket," Isabella said patiently.

"Suit yourself." Viola threw herself into a seat

with a dramatic sigh. It was also the seat with the best view of the laptop. "Ah! Where's the detonator for Russek? Someone? Yes? Detonator? Yes?"

Williams cut Drew free first, and Drew promptly took the knife and cut Russek free. Orselli took care of cutting Bishop's bonds.

"Where's the data?" Williams asked Drew.

"Mademoiselle has it," he said, examining Russek's explosive belt. "She just left." He ignored Williams swearing. "Paul, what are we going to do about this?"

"Get far away from it," Bishop said, coming up to take a look. He turned to his cousin and asked, "How'd you get here?"

"We tracked your cell phone," Orselli said, glancing around nervously.

"Bishop, take Drew out of here," Russek said. "This might be my last request."

"I won't leave you," Drew said, taking Russek's hand. "Ever."

"Excuse me," Williams broke in. "I have the gun, I'm in charge, no one is going anywhere until–"

There was a lot of running feet and banging in the stairwell. Williams grabbed Drew and put the gun to his head.

"Well, well, there you are Warren," Schweik drawled. "I knew we'd catch up to you sooner or later."

Samsa was behind his supervisor, and Romero and Carpenter were behind him. Samsa went up to Drew and asked him if he was okay and got a sketchy nod.

"We've missed the main event, Schweik," Williams said, shoving Drew at Bishop. "They're gone with the data."

"I'm taking you into custody, Williams." Carpenter flashed his FBI credential and pulled handcuffs out of his pocket. "Murder, racketeering, terrorism, espionage, treason–"

"And none of it will stick, Carpenter," Schweik cut him off. "You can charge him, but no judge will go to court against a CIA agent working in conjunction with Interpol. If all else fails, he's got diplomatic immunity from the, uh, who is it this time, Warren?"

"Iceland," Williams said testily. "They're the only country that couldn't care less about the Sirens and this crazy mess." He turned to Drew. "I'd like to show you Iceland. Come with me, I'll show you a world you never knew existed. We'll be patriots and fight world terrorism together."

"No thanks," Drew said. "I've had enough patriotism. I just want Paul and some peace."

"How boring," Williams said. "Let me know if you change your mind." He shrugged and glared at Schweik. "How'd you get here so fast, Schweik? I figured I had an hour or two head-start at least."

"We were tracking Drew here," Samsa said, pointing to the cell phone in Drew's hand. "With that."

"Clever," Williams said. "What about you FBI and DHS guys?"

"We bought Orselli a few weeks ago when we connected him to Bishop and Bishop to Russek and Ryan," Romero said, matter-of-factly. "He's been keeping tabs on you for us for a week."

"A week! We could've wrapped thi–" Russek yelled.

Matter-of-factly, Williams shot Kevin Orselli in the chest and head. "Got a problem with that, Bishop?" he asked.

"Nah. I'll have to get a new lawyer," Bishop said, looking away from his cousin's corpse. "Look, can I go back to jail now? It's a lot safer there."

"Goddamn it!" Russek yelled. "Somebody give me a phone so I can call the cops!"

Drew and Bishop simultaneously offered him phones.

"Jesus Christ! Is that a suicide bomber belt on Russek?!" Romero looked like he might faint.

"No. It isn't," Williams said bluntly.

Romero started to say something else, but all hell

broke loose just then and they were all very busy shooting, running away, and trying not to get shot.

"Why doesn't this detonator work?" Viola asked, glaring at Williams on the laptop screen.

"Because that's not C4," Kate said, patiently, closing her cell phone prior to throwing it out the window and onto the freeway. "I told you we were out of C4 and I couldn't get any."

"So what is it?" Helena asked

"It's modeling clay," Kate said. "It was the best I could do on short notice," she added when they just stared at her.

"I hope y'all're recording all this while up here I'm driving," Isabella yelled from the front seat. All she could hear was Helena roaring with laughter and Viola and Kate arguing in a language she couldn't understand, like a harem hissy fit. Then lots of shooting from the laptop speakers.

They later learned that in the firefight, Samsa and Carpenter were killed, Schweik was shot in the right thigh and ultimately lost his leg, surgeons spent several hours sewing Romero's right lung up after he was shot in the chest, and Warren Williams made like Houdini and disappeared into thin air yet again. None of the Samoan girls survived the battle once the LAPD arrived; they were flanked and outgunned. Bishop, Russek and Ryan survived by dropping to the floor and staying there until the all clear.

At Russek's suggestion, and with the watch commander's consent, Bishop slapped a patrolman and was allowed to return to the County jail for an indefinite-pending-court-date stay. Russek and Ryan went home and, as far as anyone concerned with this story knew, lived happily ever after.

Or not: once the mission was over, Titania and her group had other, more pressing, concerns than two homosexuals in Los Angeles.

Chapter 14

'Tis a Wonder, by Your Leave, She will be Tamed so.

"And now what, Department Manager?" Titania asked. She'd been prepared for a lot of things at this disciplinary meeting, but not to be sitting next to the body of her former immediate supervisor.

"Agent Titania, may I call you Titania?" he asked.

"Oh, please do."

"How long were you a government employee?" he asked.

"Twenty-seven years."

"You've been a bureaucrat your entire career?"

"Yes, I've either worked as an analyst or manager for the U.S. government or been a contractor for it for thirty-two years," she said. "One might not see much of the world in the Civil Service, but one sees deeply into our country, who really runs it, and how they run it, no matter what pay grade one is at."

"Then I suspect you've realized that the past eight years have been a mixed blessing for the espionage community and the country at large," he said wearily, as if he was, perhaps, saying this to a lot of people. "As you know, this election will likely bring fresh minds, idealistic minds, bent on change, into our government. Fresh minds that would recoil in horror at what our departments have done to fight terrorism or for other reasons, some of them quite lucrative, over the past seven years. Or, should the unthinkable be elected, we would find ourselves with an old mind and a clueless mind in the White House with no discernable agenda, and vulnerable to influences beyond our control, which are equally dangerous to our departments. Well before the inauguration of either of these horrors, my superiors and subordinates will be sanitizing records, procedures and processes, and, with mixed emotions, will return to the analysis of terrorism as opposed to its manufacture. And so, Titania, this is why I must ask you to disband your highly effective group. Of course as a private citizen and a former government contractor you may do as you please, but all record of your association with the Cheney government– I mean– well, you know what I mean, must be severed, expunged and eradicated.

"However, before this meeting I came to the conclusion that as dangerous as you are alive, you are more dangerous dead. Based on my readings of your team's missions, methods, and success rate, they are well led, which is a tribute to your organizational and leadership abilities. As the events in Irvine and Los Angeles were well orchestrated and goal-focused, the level of terror was extreme, but never out of control due to, I believe, your direction. Without you, the world would be a much more dangerous place, and it is dangerous enough as it is.

"And so I must ask you to disband your unit and retire your agents as you see fit. You will return to your operations in Maryland and my team and I will unofficially be monitoring your activities, legal and otherwise. Your cover as a financial services advisor has been very effective and since you have no team to manage, I will expect some of your off-the-books, offshore revenue to flow upstream to my projects. As you will also report to me on your former agents' whereabouts and activities in monthly reports. I'm sure their wellbeing will be an incentive to make as much money as possible for the team, my team, which you are now on. I hope we understand each other," he added with a bureaucratic smile. "Think of the next decade or so as a productive and lucrative hibernation."

"Or like cicadas," Titania said pleasantly. "Between swarms or whatever cicadas do. Yes, I understand."

His cell phone buzzed and he spoke briefly into it. "The 'cleaners' are here," he said, clicking his phone shut and nodding at her late Section Manager. "They'll take care of any fingerprints."

"I see. Well, I'll just use the bathroom and be on my way," she said, getting to her feet and picking up her briefcase. "Too many lattes."

The Department Manager was a gentleman and waited to escort her out. He didn't notice she didn't have her briefcase with her, just her purse and a portfolio under her arm. "I look forward to working with you, Titania. I think you'll like working with my people, as well," he said when they parted in the mall parking garage. "There are minds in my department that are not quite as brilliant as yours, but you might inspire them to new heights." He shook her hand and smiled almost sincerely.

Titania went to her car and drove away from the mall. At a traffic light she took an electronic device out of her purse and detonated the C4 she'd left in the ladies' room of the basement of the mall and the bomb Isabella had put in the Department Manager's car. Just to be thorough, she detonated the C4 Isabella had put in the Section Manager's car as well, even though he certainly wasn't driving it. Isabella had been happy to do these last little chores for Titania. All the Sirens had been willing to help Titania in her bureaucratic struggle session, but Isabella had arrived first and it was merely three bombs. Certainly nothing she and Titania couldn't handle easily.

After Los Angeles and examining world events and the mood of the country, Titania had come to the conclusion it was time to restructure her operations. She installed Miranda in an undisclosed secure location with all the money and technology the hacker could ever want. Miranda was keeping Electricland going, but the game was now only a game, and any data harvested would only be for her own amusement (except for what she felt Titania should know about). Hermia would run drugs and guns in South and Southeast Asia as she always had.   Kate, Helena, and Isabella settled discreetly in the United States. They were so discreetly settled that although Titania could see them collecting their stipends from her accounts, she had no idea where they were or what they were doing there. Presumably they were all in legal, even respectable, identities and living well, which is still the best revenge. Titania had dinner with Viola before driving her to the airport to return permanently to Beirut.

"Will you miss any of this?" Titania asked in the car.

"I'll miss you and the others," Viola said, leaning back in her seat, watching the traffic go by.

"But you won't miss the work?"

"No.   Los Angeles, and, to some extent, Baku burned me out," Viola said. "I've run out of ideas for destroying the world one bomb at a time. I'd just like to relax and see what happens next."

"For now," Titania said.

"For forever." She shrugged. "I think. I also miss my home and I want to rest, keep house, feel safe."

"In Beirut?"

"Safety is a state of mind, cheri," Viola said. "You be safe also."

"I will," Titania said, pulling into the airport roundabout. "No regrets?"

"None.   Eh, perhaps one." Viola looked at the woman next to her, whom she might never see again. "I regret that Warren Williams isn't dead."

"Yes, as far as we can find out, he's still alive, somewhere. But that's more of a concern than a regret, I think." Titania parked at the white curb and popped the trunk so Viola could get her suitcase out of it. They hugged under the scolding eye of parking enforcement. "Just remember, Viola, you can't win them all."

"Yes. Too bad for us. Adieu, Titania."

"Bon voyage, Viola. Adieu."

"Hey, lady!" the parking guy in a reflective vest

yelled at them. "You can't park there!"

Titania turned toward him. "Yes, just a moment." When she turned back, Viola was gone.

The End